Dedicated to Deb
You are loved
You are remembered
You are missed beyond measure

The Boy On The Side Of The Road

A NOVEL BY

TAMMI HAYNES

ddg publishing

WWW.DOODLEBUGDESIGNGROUP.NET

Fate is not an eagle. It creeps like a rat.

— Elizabeth Bowen

Chapter One

May 8, 1954, Dawson, Georgia

Six-year-old, Noah McAllister, waved enthusiastically to his best friend Curtis as the school bus pulled away belching its customary cloud of black smoke.

When the bus was out of sight he sat on the ground and pulled off his shoes. It felt good to get the ill-fitting shoes off his feet, and he smiled with pleasure as he wiggled his toes in the dirt.

Shoes was such dumb things! Why'd Aunt Rose have to go and give 'em to Momma when her boy couldn't wear 'em no more anyhow?

That train of thought lasted only a moment, and after tying the strings together he threw the shoes over his shoulder and started the quarter-mile walk home, quickly forgetting about Aunt Rose and blistered feet.

When the sweltering Georgia heat caused beads of perspiration to trickle down Noah's temple, an image of the cool waters of Muddy Creek crossed his mind. The creek reminded him that tomorrow was Saturday, which was the best day of all!

On Saturdays, after his chores where finished, Noah, Curtis, and a few others from school would go to the shallow watering hole not far from the McAllister farm where they could just hang out and have fun.

7

Yeah, Saturday sure was the best day of all!

As Noah continued toward home, something else occurred to him. He slipped his hand into the pocket of his worn-out dungarees and pulled out the neatly folded sheet of purple paper. He carefully unfolded it and stared down at the picture he'd drawn earlier in the day.

Smiling broadly, Noah recalled what his teacher, Miss Lewis had said.

"Noah, what a lovely house, and that's such a nice tree. I'm certain your mother will think it's the best Mother's Day present ever! Well done."

Someday, when I'm big, I'm gonna buy Momma a nice house like that, and all kinds of nice stuff. Even a television like the one Aunt Rose has, cuz Momma sure likes that television.

Pap don't like it much, so I'll have to buy him somethin' different. And we won't have to raise chickens no more neither. Yeah, when I'm big, we're gonna live in a house just like Aunt Rose's in Valdosta, and we'll give that stupid ol' chicken farm to somebody else ...

Lost in his private daydream, Noah didn't hear the soft whimper, or see the melon crate tucked in among the oak trees on the side of the road.

When the sound came again, he looked up from the paper and spied the crate several yards away. Haphazardly cramming his mother's gift back into his pocket, he ran excitedly toward it, then stopped a few feet short and inhaled sharply.

Peering through the space between the first and second slats were two little brown eyes. Eight tiny fingers precariously gripped the top board.

One of his father's colorful phrases came to mind, and Noah blurted out, "What the sam hell?"

Frightened by the outburst, the baby began to cry, lost his hold and landed with a thud in the middle of the crate. Noah simply stared at the little boy in awe.

When the shock of his discovery subsided, he took a hesitant step toward the child and gingerly patted him on the head.

"It's okay little fella," he said comfortingly.

Within minutes the little boy quieted, although fat tears were still glistening on his tiny face as he lifted scrawny arms up to Noah, who none too gently began to pull him from the confining space.

Suddenly, like a mighty clap of thunder an engine roared to life. Noah spun around in time to see a dark car explode from behind the trees and careen onto the road. Seconds later it was gone, leaving behind a trail of dust as the only evidence it had been there at all.

He hadn't noticed the car when he got off the bus, so he couldn't have known it had been there all along, waiting for someone, anyone, to arrive.

When the bundle he held began to squirm uncomfortably, Noah dismissed the car and its occupants and returned his attention to the child. Then with the baby awkwardly angled in his arms, he continued home, walking as quickly as his short legs would allow.

"Momma! Momma! Look what I found!" he shouted as he burst through the McAllister's front door.

In appearance, Sarah McAllister was the exact opposite of her robust, towheaded son, and stout, blue-eyed, blonde-haired husband. She had dark brown hair and gentle brown eyes, and although she was thirty-three, her slight frame and unlined features gave the impression of a much younger woman.

Hearing Noah's excited exclamations, Sarah smiled, turned from the boiling pot of potatoes on the stove and started for the living room.

However, the smile on her face quickly vanished when she saw her flush-faced son and what he had 'found.'

"Lord Almighty Noah, where on earth ..." she began.

Noah allowed the child to slide to the floor. Still beaming, he looked up at his mother and rushed on excitedly, "I found him Momma. He was just sittin' in a crate down by the trees, just sittin' there all by himself. Can I keep him? I'll take real good care of him. I promise!"

When his words finally sunk in, Sarah shook her head and said gently, "Noah. Honey. He's not a puppy, son. This child belongs to somebody. We can't just 'keep' him."

Noah burst into tears, "Somebody throwed him away Momma. I bet they don't want him no more! Please! Please let me keep him! I promise he won't be no trouble! I promise I'll take care of him!"

9

Noah had, in the innocent way of a child, worked it all out. He was always bringing home strays. Okay, so mostly they were puppies or kittens, but what difference did that make? 'Sides, finders' keepers, losers' weepers, his young mind reasoned.

Sarah was at a total loss for words as she stared at the two boys. Both were wailing loudly now.

"What the sam hell is goin' on here?" Noble McAllister bellowed as he threw open the screen door.

He had heard the commotion all the way out in his workshed and had quickly dropped what he was doing and ran to the house.

All eyes turned to him and everyone fell silent. Noble looked from Noah to the baby, then questioningly at his wife.

"Noble, look what Noah 'found' comin' home from school," she said slowly, nodding toward the little boy.

"What do you mean found?" he asked, as he wrinkled his brow in confusion.

"I did Pap! I found him in a crate just off the road. He was sittin' there all by himself! So can I keep him? Please?" Noah continued pleadingly.

Noble and Sarah exchanged a look of bewilderment.

Lifting the baseball cap from his sweaty head, Noble scratched his forehead and said, "Boy, you just don't find babies like that."

"I'm not lyin' Pap, I did find him, I swear! I'll even show ya," Noah said, grabbing his father's hand and tugging him toward the front door.

Sarah watched Noah pull his father excitedly along behind him, and for a moment stood staring after the two people she loved most in the world.

The child began to whimper then, and Sarah turned to look at the little intruder. He looked up at her with a woeful expression as he reached out his painfully thin arms, and the gesture caused a twinge of pity to wash over her.

"Come on little one. No harm in cleanin' you up I guess," she said, as she gathered him into her arms.

For the first time she noticed the disgusting condition the child was in. His only clothing was a filthy rag fashioned as a diaper, which was soaked with urine. As far as Sarah could see, there wasn't a clean spot on him.

10

She also noticed the bruise under his right eye. He seemed so small and frail, she guessed he couldn't be more than a year old.

After removing the odorous rag, she promptly walked outside and threw it in the burn barrel. Then she took the little boy into the kitchen and made a warm bath in the sink.

Once the child had been scrubbed clean and she was toweling him off, Sarah saw other bruises covering his tiny body. The abuse the child must have endured filled her mother's heart with terrible sadness. She could not fathom who, on God's green earth could mistreat a helpless baby in such a way.

Holding the little boy tenderly, she sat with him at the kitchen table and rocked him gently.

That's how Noah and his father found them when they returned.

Noble placed a comforting hand to his wife's shoulder.

Sarah looked up at him with stormy eyes full of anger, and cried out furiously, "Noble, someone has been beatin' this child. His entire little body is covered with ugly bruises. We can't let him go back to the people responsible for this. They're not fit to live!"

Noble shook his head in agreement and held out a brown cigar box.

"Sarah, our boy's tellin' the truth. It looks like somebody just stuck that kid in a crate and left him. I found this, and an old dirty blanket."

Sarah wiped her eyes with a corner of the towel she still had wrapped around the baby. Then she smoothed his hair into place and tenderly kissed the top of his small head.

She looked at Noah who had been standing quietly in the archway that connected the kitchen to the living room.

"Son, get this little one a piece of bread and take him out to the other room."

Without a word, Noah promptly obeyed.

Noble pulled out a chair, sat down across from his wife and handed her the cigar box. Sarah peeled off the tape securing the lid and opened it. Inside she found a letter written in a crude, clearly uneducated hand. The letter simply stated that the boy's name was Melvin, and he was two-years-old. No last name or date of birth was given.

After several long, silent moments, Sarah said, "Noble, I don't recall ever seein' that little boy anywhere around town. Maybe he's not even from around here, maybe his folks were just passin' through."

Noble thought about it for a moment, then recalled a couple that had recently started working at the Peterson service station in Dawson.

Harvey Peterson and his wife Edna, owned the station. They were good people, both in their late sixties. Noble would often exchange chickens and eggs for gas with the old man.

They had one full-time employee, Hudge Bueller, who was out sick more often than he actually worked. So from time to time they would take on extra help. Usually transients passing through who would work just long enough to get them to the next town.

Finally, he said, "Sarah, I think I might know who that boy belongs to, in fact, I'm pretty sure of it. That little one in there looks an awful lot like that fella I met over at the service station the other day. He was pumpin' gasoline for Harv.

"He didn't say much, just kinda kept his head down and did his job. I asked him where Harvey was at, he mumbled somethin' I couldn't quite understand then points to the office. So I go up to pay Harv for the gas and there's a girl in there sweepin' the floor. I bet she couldn've been more than sixteen if she was a day.

"Anyhow, old Harv comes walkin' in from the garage, I pay him for the gasoline and we walk back outside and he nods over at the fella and says, 'You meet my new attendant Leonard?' I say, well, I guess you could say we met. Then Harvey gets this look on his face and he says, 'That little girl in there is his wife, Missy.'

"We talked about that for a minute then I asked him where old Hudge was at."

Noble stopped, shook his head and laughed, then continued.

"He says, 'That darn fool was out huntin' and shot himself in the leg. I wouldn't be a bit surprised to find out he done it deliberate! One of these days I'm gonna fire that lazy rat, I swear!'

"Anyhow, I'll bet you a dollar to a donut that little boy belongs to that couple. I suspect they're long gone by now, but I'll go on over there and talk to Harv. See what I can find out."

Sarah was quiet for a moment, then said, "Okay Noble, but if they're not there, don't say anything about the baby yet ... please?"

Noble felt a little uneasy about his wife's request, but decided he would at least hear what the Petersons had to say before he mentioned that Sarah and he may have Leonard and Missy's child.

As soon as Noble left the house, Noah approached his mother who was still seated at the table, "So can I keep 'im Momma?"

Smiling warmly, she stretched out her arms, "C'mere son."

After he climbed onto her lap she hugged him tightly, "I really don't know what's gonna happen yet."

Noah looked up at his mother and as Sarah stared into her son's beautiful cerulean blue eyes, she was struck by a premonition of looming disaster. She quickly said a prayer for God to protect her family from whatever harm might be headed their way.

"But if nobody wants him, I can keep 'im, huh Momma?" her tenacious six-year-old was saying as she finished her ardent plea.

'If nobody wants him.' Sarah found Noah's innocent acceptance that someone could so easily discard a child in such a way, sadly amusing.

Just then the hissing sound of water boiling over reminded her of the potatoes on the stove and the chicken in the oven.

Setting Noah away from her, she said, "Why don't you go keep an eye on that little one son so I can finish makin' supper?"

"Okay Momma," Noah said cheerfully as he skipped out of the room.

While Sarah finished preparing her family's supper, that intense feeling of impending disaster continued to plague her.

When Noble pulled into the station, even before he got out of the truck, he sensed something was wrong. Aside from the fact that no one came out to greet him, which was unusual in itself, the garage doors were closed.

It was far too hot and humid to work on cars with them shut, and Noble couldn't recall Harvey ever having them down during business hours. Also, there was an odd stillness in the air. No singing birds, no chirping crickets — nothing but dead silence.

For several seconds Noble sat motionless in the pick-up as a knot of apprehension twisted in the pit of his stomach. All of a sudden, he felt a prickly sensation on the back of his neck and swiped at it in agitation.

The feeling of unease was so strong he briefly thought about slamming the truck in reverse and heading straight for the sheriff's office.

Yet, he hesitated, and after a moment chided himself for being foolish, shut off the engine and jumped out of the pick-up.

"Harv?" he called out.

Nothing.

He walked cautiously around to the front of the truck and called out a second time.

Still nothing.

There it was again. That feeling of someone sneaking up behind him, and he slapped at the back of his neck a second time.

Noble put his hands to his hips and shook his head, then walked over to the office. The 'Closed' sign could barely be seen through the dirty window even up close.

Noble had never known Harvey to close up shop early. In fact, Harvey Peterson kept to such a strict schedule you could set your clocks by him. He opened every morning promptly at seven, Monday through Saturday. He would close up at one, walk across the street to his house, have lunch with Edna, promptly open again at two, then close for the day at six p.m. sharp.

Noble wiped at the grimy window, placed his hands to either side of his face and peered inside. Everything looked okay as far as he could tell, so he turned from the window and looked out across the street to the Peterson house. Harvey and Edna's blue Ford was sitting in the driveway, and the ordinary, familiar sight calmed his frayed nerves a little.

"Shoot, maybe the old man decided to finally take a day off," Noble said aloud, and relieved that there could be a normal explanation for all of this, decided to just go home.

But as he walked back to the pick-up and opened the door, he remembered what had brought him here in the first place — the boy Noah had found. He slammed the door soundly, mumbled irritably under his breath, then headed across the street to the house.

The Petersons lived and worked at the southern end of Dawson. A mile from their closest neighbor, and a mile and a half from what the locals referred to as 'downtown,' which was really nothing more than a few scattered businesses on either side of the street.

On one side there was Doc Hadley's office, a barber shop, Oliver and Maria Hernandez' grocery store, Simmon's Hardware, and Ida's Cafe.

On the other side, the sheriff's office, a consignment store which sold everything from knickknacks to used clothing, furniture, and even small farming equipment, an apothecary, and at the very northern end, right across the street from one another sat the Dawson Baptist Church and Farley's Funeral Home.

For some reason, the fact that Dawson, with a population of less than three hundred people had a funeral home, always tickled Noble's funnybone. Business couldn't be good, yet somehow they had managed to stay in operation almost as long as the town itself had been in existence.

Aside from Sunday services and an occasional dinner at Ida's Cafe, the McAllisters didn't socialize much. However, in the ten years they had been residents of the small community, they had come to know just about everyone who lived in town, and most who lived on the surrounding farms, mainly through selling chickens.

It was a quiet place. A good place to raise a family.

The closer Noble got to the house, the faster his heart began to pound, and the more convinced he became that something was truly wrong. Like the front gate — it was wide open. The Petersons would never have left it unlatched, let alone open, because their beloved dog Mitzy would have gotten out of the yard.

Mitzy was nowhere in sight.

Then there was Harvey's work boots — one was by the door, the other lay on its side at the bottom of the porch steps.

That was another thing. The Peterson house, unlike their service station, was meticulously kept, inside and out, and Edna was fanatical about everything having its proper place and being there at all times.

She never allowed Harvey to wear his greasy work boots in the house. So he always took them off before entering and placed them neatly by the front door.

Noble latched the gate behind him and continued down the

short walkway to the house. When he reached the porch, he picked up the boot, climbed the steps, walked over and sat it down beside its partner. That's when he noticed the sticky shoe imprints.

He brushed across one with his shoe, smearing it, which caused him to conclude that whatever the dark substance was, it couldn't have been there very long.

Then he stepped up to the door and gave it several rapid taps, waited a few seconds, then knocked again, this time a little harder — nothing.

He lifted his baseball cap and scratched the top of his head.

"Harvey? Miz Edna?. . .You in there?"

He cocked his head to one side and listened intently — dead silence.

"What the sam hell is goin' on here?" he muttered half aloud.

"I have had just about all the nonsense I can take for one day!" Noble spat out angrily.

Then he tried the knob, when it turned easily under his hand, he pushed the door open a couple of inches and called out a little more gruffly, "Miz Edna? ... Harvey?"

When there was still no response he pushed the door open wide and stepped over the threshold. And just as he stepped through the doorway he saw it — but for a fraction of a second his mind simply could not comprehend what his eyes were recording.

There was blood splattered everywhere he looked.

"Oh, Sweet Jesus!" Noble groaned at the same time an explosion of shear terror ripped through his chest.

"Harvey! Edna!" Noble shouted forcefully, as he continued forward on legs that threatened to buckle beneath him.

He nearly blacked out from shock, and for a moment had to stand statue still as the room slowly came back into focus. That's when he saw Harvey's lifeless body lying halfway between the living room and the kitchen. As he catapulted forward, he tripped over something, and fell heavily to his knees.

He jerked his head back sharply toward the door and saw it was Mitzy he had tripped over. Her white fur was soaked in crimson blood, a maniacal snarl frozen on her face. Noble turned away quickly and crawled the remaining distance to where Harvey lay face-down.

When he turned him onto his back, his stomach convulsed in a wave of nausea. Harvey's face had been pulverized to such an extent that he was unrecognizable. Nothing remained but a mass of mangled flesh and broken bones, leaving no doubt that he was dead.

"Lordy! Lordy! Who did this?" Noble cried out in disbelief.

Reeling, he swallowed back the bile in his throat and leaning heavily against the wall, pushed himself shakily to his feet. Now he saw that Edna lay not more than five feet from her husband on the kitchen floor, halfway under the dining table.

Noble pushed the table out of the way and knelt beside the elderly woman. Although she didn't appear to be as badly beaten as Harvey, he was certain she was just as dead.

Then Edna moaned softly, and Noble, without hesitation, sprang into action. As gently as he could, he rolled her onto her back and began to wipe the blood from her eyes with his shirt-tail.

"Oh, Thank You Jesus! Hold on Miz Edna! Hold on! I'm gonna get help. You just hold on now," he spewed encouragingly as he frantically looked around the room for the phone.

Noble quickly found it and dialed the sheriff.

When he heard Beth's friendly voice at the other end say, "Sheriff's office," he breathed a huge sigh of relief.

"Beth! Get Ernest, get the Doc, tell them to get over to the Petersons right now!" Noble ranted into the receiver.

"Mr. McAllister?" Beth asked confused.

"Yes! Yes! It's me! Now tell them to get over here!"

"What's happened? What's wrong?"

"There isn't time to explain! Just tell 'em to come quick before it's too late ... Do it now!" Noble shouted furiously.

"Well, Mr. McAllister ... Sheriff Tipton isn't here, but I'll radio ..." Beth began nervously.

"Oh, for the love of ..." Noble hissed.

"Oh, wait a minute here he comes," she interrupted as Ernest suddenly stepped through the doorway.

At the perplexed look on the receptionist's face, Tipton pointed to the phone questioningly.

Beth shrugged her shoulders, held the receiver out to him and said, "It's Noble McAllister ... somethin's goin' on out at the Peterson place."

Tipton snatched the phone from Beth's hand and said gruffly, "Sheriff Tipton here."

"Ernest, you gotta get Ben Hadley over here to the Petersons quick!"

"Why? What's goin' on?"

"Oh Lord have mercy, somethin' awful's happened! And if you don't get Ben out here in a hurry it's gonna be too late! Miz Edna ain't gonna make it!" Noble yelled, frustrated that precious minutes were slipping by while Edna lay dying.

"Now just hold on boy! I'm not goin' anywhere 'till I know what the hell you're goin' on about!"

"There's no time! Just get Hadley out here *NOW!*" Noble screamed, then slammed the receiver down, wishing it were physically possible to reach through the line and ring Tipton's neck.

He raced back to Edna, and for the span of a heartbeat, believed it was already too late. But then she coughed, oozing bloody spittle from her broken lips. Noble quickly grabbed the bottom of his shirt again, sank to his knees beside her and began to tenderly wipe the blood from her swollen mouth.

"Hang on Miz Edna, help's comin'. Doc Hadley's gonna be here in no time. Now you just hold on ol' girl."

Agonizing seconds ticked by and no one came. Then minutes, as he sat there helplessly, literally watching the life drain out of the poor old woman's body.

Finally, after what seemed like a lifetime to Noble, help arrived.

Tipton stood at the open doorway, his face the color of newly fallen snow as he surveyed the horror before him. Like Noble moments earlier, his stomach convulsed with nausea, and, unable to control himself, he doubled over and vomited.

Once he recovered, he stammered, "I ... I ... what happened here ..."

"Ben. Ernest. We're in here," Noble shouted from the kitchen.

Ernest didn't say anything as he cautiously maneuvered across the blood stained floor, gingerly stepping over Harvey as he made his way to Noble and Edna.

When Noble saw that Tipton was alone, he shouted incredulously, "Where the *hell* is Ben?"

"Noble, I ... I had no idea ..." Earnest began awkwardly again.

Cutting him off abruptly, Noble ground out slowly, "Ernest! Where is Dr. Hadley?"

"He, he ... ain't comin'. I ... I didn't call him."

Shaking with rage, Noble screamed, "WHAT!"

"Listen Noble, I couldn't go gettin' the whole dang town in an uproar over a phone call I couldn't make no sense of! I never dreamed ..." Ernest whined.

"Well get on the phone and get him out here *NOW!*" Noble barked furiously.

"No, no it'll be faster if we take her to him in the squad car," Ernest offered.

Noble glared at him accusingly, as Tipton bent down to help lift Edna gently off the floor.

It is curious that physical courage should be so common in the world and moral courage so rare.

— Mark Twain

Chapter Two

With the siren blaring, Ernest pulled to a screeching halt in front of Dr. Hadley's office. The noise alone was enough to stop people on the street and bring them out of their shops to see what was causing all the commotion.

Noble, holding Edna gingerly in his arms, emerged from the car before Ernest had a chance to help them.

As Noble carried the battered woman around the car and to the sidewalk, those close enough to see, gasped in horror. One woman, Maude Grimes, screamed, which brought nearly everyone within ear shot running to get a closer look as to the cause of her distress.

Suddenly the walkway in front of Hadley's clinic became so crowded, Ernest had to shout for everyone to step back and make room so Noble could get Edna inside.

Once Edna was in Ben's capable hands, Noble breathed a huge sigh of relief.

As Doc Hadley and his efficient nurse, Josephine, went to work, Noble realized there was nothing more he could do to help, so he left the doctor and his assistant to tend to Edna and went back outside.

Ernest was still trying unsuccessfully to quiet the growing crowd.

Eventually, the noise died down and Ernest said, "Folks, this is bad, this is real bad. Old Harvey Peterson's been murdered, and Edna nearly too."

The crowd exploded with cries of outrage.

"How?"

"Who did it?"

"Where's Harv now?"

"Where's that lowlife Bueller at?"

Questions, like bullets in a shoot-out, were flying at Tipton from every direction.

The only two he could answer with any confidence were, "Harvey's still at the house and Hudge is laid up from shootin' himself in the leg. I saw him myself this afternoon, so don't go gettin' any ideas," Earnest warned.

Someone shouted, "Where's those folks that's been hangin' around Harv's station?"

With that simple question everything changed. Suddenly, Ernest was faced with an unruly mob bent on vengeance. Having never faced a situation like this before, it was difficult for the small town sheriff to keep a clear thought in his head, let alone decide what to do next.

So before he knew it, the men from Dawson, including himself, were scrambling to their cars to find the "murderin' lowlifes" responsible for the heinous crime committed against the Petersons.

Noble, bone weary and emotionally drained, had been quietly resting against the wall watching the crowd turn from concerned citizens to vigilantes in a blink of an eye. With growing dread, he couldn't help but wonder what more this God forsaken day had in store for them.

As Ernest started to get in his squad car, he spied Noble, and shouted, "Come on Noble, you ride with me."

"I'm not goin' anywhere but home Ernest," Noble replied flatly.

"Like hell you are! We're gonna need all the help we can get if we're gonna catch those murderin' skunks that killed poor old Harv."

Noble sighed heavily, walked over to the squad car and got in.

"Did you see those folks anywhere around when you got to the station?" Ernest asked as they led the pack out of town.

"Nope. Place was closed up when I got there."

"Well, Mason, Newton, and Leon's gonna go get Harvey and take him to the funeral home. Then catch up with us," Ernest continued.

Noble didn't say anything as an image of Harvey's bloody, disfigured face, filled his mind.

After scouring the surrounding area for several hours, the men from Dawson found no trace of the drifters. And with the sun beginning to set, it was decided to head back into town and begin again at daybreak.

Then all of a sudden, Dewey Johnson stopped in the middle of the road and started banging loudly on the outside of his pick-up door.

He jumped out shouting "Over there, over there!" and began pointing wildly off into the distance, where the outline of a vehicle could barely be seen among the trees.

When the others could see what he was going on about, they quickly turned around and sped toward Butcher Road.

Within minutes, they had the couple, who were indeed the same two from Harvey's station, surrounded. The man, Leonard, was standing in front of the disabled Buick with the hood up, fear contorted his face.

The girl was sitting behind the steering wheel. Her luminous eyes were filled with stark terror.

"Hey! They got stuff in here b'longs to Harv and Edna!" Dirk Wittley shouted as he peered into the back seat of the car.

All of a sudden the men moved in closer and began shouting obscenities at the two outsiders. Ernest, fearful that the situation was about to get even uglier, awkwardly yanked his gun from its holster, and began waving it around nervously as he shouted for everyone to calm down and step back. Then he ordered the girl out of the vehicle.

Just as she stepped away from the car, the gun went off, and in a split second she crumpled to the ground.

Momentarily stunned, everyone stared down at the fallen woman as a dark pool of blood began to slowly seep out around her mid-section.

Seizing his chance, Leonard made a run for it, but the men of Dawson were upon him in seconds, and like a pack of wild dogs began a brutal assault.

As soon as Noble heard the sickening, bone-crushing thwack of fist meeting flesh as someone slugged Leonard squarely in the face, he knew the man would be dead within minutes if somebody didn't step in. Though he felt no pity for the killer, in his book, two wrongs did not make a right.

He frantically looked around him for help of any kind and caught sight of Ernest, who was still staring blankly down at the dead woman, his gun hanging limply from his right hand at his side. Then he spied Jess Spencer and George Scott standing just outside the meleé. Both appeared to be as much in shock as Ernest was, so Noble, terrified to the bone, did the only thing his conscience would allow — he charged into the fray, shouting, "Stop this! Stop this! You're gonna kill him!"

Almost instantly Noble took a blow to the side of his head that dropped him to his knees, and before he could recover, he found himself hurling through the air like a missile. He hit the ground so hard it knocked the breath out of him.

Once he was able to suck precious air back into his lungs, he rolled onto his stomach and tried to rise to his hands and knees, only to fall face down in the dirt again. That's when Jess and George rushed to his side and began to help him up.

Just as Noble got to his feet, everything went quiet. An eerie silence and overpowering stench of blood and sweat permeated the thick air.

After a few moments, the mob backed away from Leonard, who was lying motionless on the ground.

By then Ernest had recovered enough to walk over to where the man lay sprawled.

He bent down, checked his pulse, then stood up and declared nervously, "Well, we're really in it now boys. They're both dead."

No one said a word for what felt like an eternity to Noble.

Then Red Dulleen whined, "We only done to them what they done to poor old Harv and Miz Edna."

No one else spoke for several more seconds.

Finally, Ernest said decisively, "That's right. That's right.

"I'd say justice's been done here tonight boys. After all, doesn't it say in the good book an eye for an eye? — You bet it does. And that's all that happened here — nothin' more."

Feeling more confident, he continued, "So here's what we're gonna do. Noble, you and Denton are gonna go get shovels. Go to Denton's place, it's the closest. Red, you and Hank are gonna tow this here car over to the lake, run it off of Sullivan's cliff, the water's deepest there. But first, we're gonna get everything out of that car and we're gonna bury it with those murderin' lowlifes, includin' the stuff they took from poor old Harv and Edna."

Silently the men began doing Ernest's bidding, including Noble, Jess, and George. Mainly, because it was just too late to do anything else.

Noble found it remarkable that Tipton, who only moments ago had been so completely useless, was now barking orders like a drill sergeant. It also occurred to him that from the moment Ernest had shown up at the Peterson home, he could be counted on the least when it counted the most.

If he had acted with any sense at all from the get-go, none of them would be here now trying to cover-up these two murders, for which they were all guilty of, rather they had participated or not, Noble reasoned.

After everything had been disposed of and all of the men came back together, Ernest had a few parting words.

He looked around the group and said, "I want you all to listen up. I want everybody to go home and forget about what was done here tonight. Right or wrong it can't be undone now. Don't even talk about it to your families. Best thing to do is just go on home and pretend it never happened. Understand?"

No one said a word.

Except Noble, who snorted in absolute disgust.

Ernest looked at him sharply, "Noble, you got somethin' you wanna say?"

"No Ernest, I don't expect I do. Like you said, it's way too late now anyhow."

"Good. Then we're all in agreement. Come on Noble, I'll give you a lift back to your pick-up."

As soon as Noble got in the squad car, Ernest began, "Noble, look ..." but before he could finish his sentence, Noble snapped, "Shut up Ernest. Just shut up."

They drove in silence the rest of the way.

It was well past midnight when Noble returned home. At first, Sarah didn't notice the blood on his clothes, because all she could focus in on was the tortured look on his ashen face.

"What happened Noble? What is it?" she asked as icy fingers of dread crawled up her spine.

Before answering, Noble asked, "Where's that boy Noah found?"

"In bed asleep. They're both in bed asleep," she answered uneasily.

"Sarah, somethin' awful's happened. Nobody was at the service station when I got there. I saw Harvey's Ford in the driveway so I walked on over to the house ...

"Sarah, somebody beat poor old Harvey to death, and Miz Edna's in real bad shape."

"Lord Almighty!" Sarah whispered, covering her mouth in shock.

"That isn't the half of it. I called Ernest and as we we're takin' Miz Edna into Doc Hadley's, it was like half the dang town showed up. People were outside Ben's clinic screamin' and yellin'. Somebody asked about them folks from the station.

"Next thing I know a bunch of us are headed out to look for that couple that had been workin' for Harv.

"Oh Sarah, we found 'em out on Butcher Road. Their car had broken down. They had some stuff somebody said belonged to Harv and Miz Edna.

"I'm not sure how it happened, but all of sudden Ernest's gun goes off and then that girl's lyin' on the ground dead. That's when the fella, Leonard, tried to make a run for it. Everybody went crazy then, and beat that man to death!

"Then Ernest comes up with this idea to bury 'em out there near Butcher Road and get rid of the evidence. After that he says, 'Go on home to your families boys and forget about what happened here tonight.' So that's what we did. We all just went home." Noble finished softly, hanging his head in shame.

"Noble, you didn't. . ." Sarah whispered in disbelief.

Noble's head jerked up and he said defensively, "No! No! I didn't touch 'em. In fact, I tried to stop 'em. And let me tell you somethin' Sarah, you were almost made a widow tonight because of it.

"Those men were crazy, they were like a pack of wild dogs tearin' and punchin' and beatin' that man. I have never seen anything like it in my whole life, and as long as God keeps me on this earth I hope I never see anything like it again!"

"What about the boy Noble? Did you say anything about the boy?" Sarah asked anxiously.

"Sar, once I opened the door at Harvey and Miz Edna's, I didn't give that boy another thought until just now when I came in the house, and that's the truth.

"I don't think anybody knows they had a kid. Nobody seemed to know much about 'em at all, not even where they were stayin'. But Sarah listen to me — that boy cannot stay here. We have got to get rid of him before anyone finds out who he is," Noble finished solemnly.

"Well ... what're we gonna do with him Noble?"

"I don't know yet, all I'm sayin' is don't get your heart set on keepin' him."

"Noble, why don't we sleep on it. We'll be able to think clearer once we've had some sleep. Maybe it'll all look differently tomorrow," Sarah said, forcing herself to speak with a calmness she in no way felt.

"I kept a plate of supper warm for you. Do you want it now."

"I ain't hungry. Throw it away." Noble said as his stomach recoiled in revulsion at the mere mention of food.

Before going to bed, Sarah went into Noah's room to check on the boys and found her son lying in bed awake. She sat down beside him and ran her fingers lovingly through his thick blonde hair.

Noah looked at the little boy who was sound asleep, "Did Pap say I could keep him Momma?"

Sarah spoke softly, "Son, it's hard to say what's gonna happen. But 'til we figure it out I want you to promise me somethin', and it's real important okay?"

At Noah's nod she continued, "You can't tell anybody about this baby. Not even Curtis, all right?"

"I promise Momma. I promise I won't tell nobody," he said earnestly.

"That's my good boy," she said. Then she kissed him on the forehead and wished him a good night.

Later, after she and Noble had gone to bed, Noah crept quietly into their room.

"Momma?" he whispered, standing at the door.

"What is it son?" Sarah asked breathlessly, nearly choking on fear.

She relaxed a little as Noah walked toward her and said, "I forgot, I made somethin' for you in school today," holding out the crumpled sheet of purple paper.

Sarah threw off the thin blanket and swung her legs over the side of the bed. The full moon cast a warm glow through the faded, weather worn curtains, which allowed enough light to see Noah's gift.

It was a yellow house with a red chimney, from which black crayon smoke curled up into the sky, and there was a big green tree in the front yard.

Sarah gave her son a heartfelt smile and said, "Well if that isn't the prettiest thing I've ever seen. You must've worked real hard on this son."

Beaming with pride, Noah pointed to the house and whispered, "Look Momma, that's yellow, just like Aunt Rose's."

Then he looked at his mother seriously, "Someday Momma, when I'm big, I'm gonna get you a house just like that, you wait and see. I promise."

Swallowing the lump in her throat, Sarah said, "You're the sweetest boy in the whole world son," then she led him back to bed.

The tragedy of life is what dies inside a man while he lives.

— Albert Schweitzer

Chapter Three

The McAllisters awoke early the next morning to a loud banging on the door. After exchanging a look of dread with his wife, Noble jumped up, pulled on his dungarees and bellowed, "Lord Almighty!" as he all but ran to the front door. Sarah, nearly frozen with terror, grabbed her tattered robe and followed after him.

When Noble yanked the door open to Denton Murphy, Sarah's eyes widened in shock. He looked like a man that had surely lost his mind. His long, thin, ferret-like face, white as flour, was pinched in fear, and his eyes, oh Lord, his eyes, red rimmed and bulging, would haunt her sleep for some time to come.

Denton stood at the door nervously shifting his feet, spewing words that made little sense.

"She's dead! She's dead! The boys are comin'! Lordy! Lordy! We're done for Noble, we're done for!" Then he spotted Sarah just behind her husband and fell silent.

After a moment of indecision, he dipped his head in greeting, "Miz Sarah," and then, "Noble we gotta talk."

Noble glanced back at his wife and nodded, then pulled the door closed behind him and followed Denton to his truck. For a moment, Sarah stood at the window wringing her hands anxiously as she peered through the curtains.

Denton frantically paced back and forth in front of Noble as he waved his arms wildly in the air.

Although Murphy's voice rose in fear, they were still too far away for her to hear clearly.

Suddenly, the pitter-patter of tiny feet behind her made Sarah's blood run cold and a new fear caused her heart to constrict painfully. She turned to find Noah, rubbing the sleep from his eyes, holding tightly to the baby's hand beside him.

Lord Almighty, what if Denton finds out about this baby? What if he finds out it belongs to those poor folks that was murdered last night? What if he tells? Lord Almighty, what's gonna happen then? Sarah's frightened mind rambled.

"What's the matter Momma? What's wrong?" Noah asked, feeling the tension in the air.

Sarah dashed to the children, swept the baby up into her arms and grabbed Noah's hand, then rushed them to the bedroom.

"Nothin' son. Nothin's wrong, we just gotta be real quiet 'til your Pap comes back in, okay?" she said breathlessly.

"How come Momma?"

"Cuz I said boy, that's all!" she snapped.

When tears welled up in Noah's eyes, Sarah instantly regretted her harshness.

Giving him a weak smile, she said gently, "Just do it cuz I told you, okay Noah?"

"Lordy! Lordy! Noble, Miz Edna, she didn't make it. She died this mornin'. I don't know who called 'em, but now there's men comin' down from Atlanta. Ernest says they're comin' down to investigate the murders. He says we all gotta meet out at Carter's farm 'fore they get here so we can get our story straight. He says you gotta come now Noble!" Murphy finished in one breath.

Noble scratched his head and let out a long, slow sigh.

"Jesus, Joseph, and Mary!" he hissed between clenched teeth, then, "Go on back and tell 'em I'm comin', I'll catch up with you shortly."

Noble watched Denton tear off down the road. Wiping a nervous hand across his face, he wondered again how in the sam hell he had gotten mixed up in this nightmare.

When Sarah heard the front door slam shut she poked her head out of the room and let out her breath, relieved to see Noble was alone.

Glancing back at her son, she said, "Stay here with the boy Noah," then quickly shut the door behind her and hurried out to her husband.

"What is it? What's happened now?"

"Sarah, Denton says Ernest Tipton wants everybody that was there last night to meet him at Carter's farm. Seems people from Atlanta's comin' down to investigate the Peterson murders."

"... Miz Edna died then?" Sarah asked weakly.

Noble nodded. "I gotta get on over there now," he said as he pulled on his shoes and grabbed his shirt from the back of the chair.

Noble was the last person to show up at Carter's that morning. And the sight that met him was anything but reassuring.

Nineteen desperate men were all talking at once. The scene reminded him of chickens running in circles after their heads had been recently lopped off.

When Ernest spied Noble, he quipped irritably, "What took you so long?" Causing everyone to turn toward him.

Noble didn't say anything as he took a seat between George Scott and Denton Murphy.

"We got some real trouble here boys. When Edna died early this morning, Ben Hadley called the authorities over in Atlanta. I don't know why he didn't call me first, but that ain't here nor there. Now it seems they're comin' down to investigate the Peterson murders," Ernest said nervously.

"Noble, they're gonna wanna talk to you ..."

"Why me?" Noble snapped furiously.

"Because you were the one to find Harv and Edna."

"Now like I was sayin', they're probably gonna wanna talk to Noble, but I think we might be able to keep everyone else out of it. Nobody needs to know anything about those drifters. The less people they have to talk to, the better I say ..."

Before Ernest could continue, Raif Watson spoke up and said, "Ernest, how're you gonna keep us out of it? The whole dang town knows we went out lookin' for those folks?"

"I know that Raif, but I have a plan. As the sheriff, I'm gonna tell those boys ..." Ernest began again.

"Ernest Tipton, you ain't got the brains God gave a piss ant!" Jess Spencer hissed.

"Sheriff! Ha! Lord Almighty man, the worst crime you ever had to solve in this two-bit town was when those Callahan boys threw a rock through Ida's cafe window! Honestly, for once in your sorry life use your head man!

"You think you're gonna just waltz up to those men from Atlanta, introduce yourself as sheriff, tell them you're handlin' things and they're gonna accept that and go on back to Atlanta none the wiser?"

Jess looked around the room and glared at every man that had taken part in the previous night's insanity.

"You all make me sick! Ernest you most of all! If you had handled this like a real sheriff, none of us would be here right now. And those two murderin' drifters would be sittin' in a jail cell where they belong!

"But I guess that ain't here nor there. So here's what I say we do — we stick to the truth as much as we can. We'll tell those boys from Atlanta Ernest organized a search party to go find those drifters. Then we'll say we never found 'em, so Ernest, you called it off around eleven p.m. and sent everybody home. Maybe, just maybe if we stick to that story we just might get through this awful thing this brainless turd of a sheriff's gotten us into!"

Everyone spoke up in agreement, and so it seemed the matter was settled.

With the meeting over, there was nothing left for the men to do but return home and wait.

As Noble got into his pick-up, Ernest called across the yard, "Noble, you got a telephone out to your place yet?"

"Nope."

"Then you better come on back into town with me so you can be there when those men get in."

"Ernest, I got things to take care of. I'll be into town shortly," Noble threw over his shoulder as he walked toward his truck.

Then he got in, and without a backward glance, tore out of the Carter's driveway.

By the time Noble returned to the farm, Noah had already fed the chickens and was watering his mother's garden as she had asked him to. When he spied his father coming up the road, he ran up to the pick-up and waited for Noble to get out.

"Pap, I already fed the chickens and I'm almost done waterin' the garden, so can I go meet the fellas down at the creek now?"

Noble looked down at his son with a scowl. "Boy, you ain't goin' nowheres today. When you're finished waterin' them vegetables, find somethin' else to do around this God forsaken farm!"

Noah's lower lip quivered pitifully and his eyes filled with tears as he watched his father stride angrily toward the house.

What'd I do to make Pap so mad? he wondered. I ain't never seen Pap look so mean, nor talk so mean like that.

Noble walked into the house to find Sarah sitting on the floor playing with the little boy. He couldn't say why for sure, but the sight fueled his already explosive anger.

Sarah was still smiling when she turned to Noble, but the look on his face quickly caused her smile to vanish.

"Sarah, what the sam hell are you doin'?"

"What do you mean Noble? I'm not doin' anything," she answered.

Noble shook his head, then sat on the sofa and scratched his brow.

Leaning forward with his elbows planted on his knees, he said heatedly, "We gotta get rid of that boy Sarah. We're already in a whole mess of trouble cuz of him."

Sarah stared as though her husband had suddenly sprouted horns.

"Noble McAllister you're not sayin' this baby's to blame for what happened yesterday are you?"

"I am! If that boy of ours hadn't brought this one here home, I never would've gone into town yesterday. Then somebody else would've found the Petersons!

"Now I have to go talk to those men from Atlanta and explain to them why I was at the Peterson house yesterday. What do you think I'm gonna tell 'em? What do you think they're gonna say if they find out — and they will! That we have the boy of the folks who murdered the Petersons? You think they're gonna believe a cockamamy story about findin' him on the side of the road?"

37

"Do you hear yourself Noble? Do you hear what you're sayin'? It's not this baby's fault nor Noah's because twenty grown men took the law into their own hands and killed this little one's family."

Unfortunately, Noah chose that very moment to walk in on his parents conversation. Still angry, still scared, Noble bellowed, "Get on outta here boy and find somethin' to do like I told ya!"

Noah burst into tears and ran back outside. The baby also began to cry and Sarah, stunned by Noble's outburst, glared at him accusingly.

Without another word, Noble jumped up from the sofa and stormed out of the house. A moment later Sarah heard the pick-up tear out of the driveway. With a heavy sigh, she gathered the baby into her arms and went outside to find Noah. He was sitting behind the house with his face in his hands, sobbing loudly.

"Son, your Pap's gone now. Why don't you come on back to the house so we can talk?" she prodded gently.

Noah looked up at his mother and hiccupped, "What'd I do Momma? What'd I do to make Pap so mad at me?"

Sarah shook her head sadly, and said, "C'mon son."

Looking like the weight of the world was on top of him, Noah hung his head and shuffled back to the house.

Sarah sat him down at the kitchen table and began, "Noah, your Pap's not mad at you ... he's just ... he's just real scared right now. And sometimes, when people are real scared, they do things they don't mean to do."

Noah's eyes widened in disbelief. That couldn't be true, cuz his Pap wasn't scared of nothin'. No, he must've done somethin' wrong, he must've!

"You understand what I'm sayin'?"

He didn't, but asked, "What's Pap scared of Momma?"

"Well. . .he's scared cuz he doesn't know what to do about this little boy."

That was as far into this nightmare as she was prepared to go with her six-year-old son.

She was greatly relieved when his face lit up and he said, "Oh! That's okay Momma, Pap don't have to do nothin' cuz I'm gonna take care of him. Tell Pap he doesn't have to be scared no more, I'll take good care of him. I promise!"

Sarah smiled indulgently at her son. If it were only that simple, she thought wistfully.

"I'll tell him son. Why don't you go on down to the creek now, Curtis and those other boys will probably be waitin' for you."

Noah jumped up grinning and started to skip out of the room, then he stopped. Frowning, he looked back at his mother, and said, "Pap said I couldn't go to the creek today."

Winking conspiratorially, Sarah said, "I'll fix it with your Pap. Just be home before supper. And Noah — remember, don't say anything about this boy."

"Okay Momma," Noah replied happily.

As agonizing hour after agonizing hour passed, the knot in Sarah's stomach grew more intense. By the time Noble returned, which was late into the evening, Sarah's nerves were raw. Overwhelmed with relief at the sight of him, she ran into his arms and hugged him tightly.

"Oh Noble, I was so scared," she whispered.

When Noble didn't respond, she stood apart from him and looked at his haggard, weary face.

"More bad news?"

Noble hung his head and shook it.

"Sarah, I want you to sit down here and listen to me, listen to me real good, okay?

"I think those fellas from Atlanta think maybe I had somethin' to do with what happened to the Petersons yesterday ..."

"What!" Sarah nearly shouted hysterically.

"That's right. They were askin' all kinds of questions Sar. Like how long have I known the Petersons, why was I at their house yesterday, things like that. I told 'em just like it happened, except why I went there in the first place — I just said I stopped by to get gasoline. I don't think they believed me though."

"Why wouldn't they believe that Noble? It is a service station?" Sarah interrupted.

"Well, I think Ernest might have had somethin' to do with that. In fact, I think that snivelin' little wart is gonna try to pin this whole thing on me."

"Noble, how can that be? He knows you could tell those men everything, especially what part he had to play in it all."

"Well, I thought about that. But like I said earlier, how's it gonna look when those men find out about that boy and who he belongs to? And didn't tell anybody? Now who do you think they're gonna believe? huh?

"Now I don't know what's in Ernest's mind that he thinks he could get away with pinnin' this on me, but here's what he did — when I said I was at the station to get gasoline, he leans back in his chair, puffs himself up like a peacock and says, 'You still tradin' chickens for gasoline?' I said 'yeah, sometimes.' Then he leans over and says, 'You didn't have no chickens in the back of that pick-up truck yesterday!'

"You see what I'm tellin' you Sarah?"

"Noble, there were what? Eighteen, nineteen or so other men there last night, besides you and Ernest? Not to mention, you were the one to call for help when you found Harvey and Miz Edna. And didn't you say you talked to Beth when you called the sheriff? — that makes twenty, twenty-one.

What I'm sayin' is there are just too many people who know what really happened at least to those drifters for Ernest to. . . ."

"Oh yeah? You weren't there last night. You didn't see what those men did to that Leonard. You didn't see 'em this morning — they're scared out of their minds. Cuz they know if those fellas from Atlanta find out what happened, they're all goin' to jail.

"Now, most of 'em are good men. I'd say most of 'em never did a dishonest thing in their lives before yesterday. But if it comes down to it, they'll hang me out to dry if it means savin' their own necks, especially when they find out that we had that little boy, who by the way, looks just like that Leonard, all this time and didn't tell anyone.

"Don't you think that makes us look a little suspicious? Like maybe we were in cahoots with 'em or somethin'? Shoot, I know that's what I'd think.

"The only thing I can see to do here, is get rid of that boy. Now! Tonight! Then I think I'll at least have a fightin' chance to explain myself if need be."

Sarah stared unblinkingly at Noble for a long moment.

"What do you mean "get rid of him"?" she asked slowly.

"I mean we take that boy somewhere and drop him off just like his own people did!"

Sarah felt a heavy coldness creep into her heart.

"Noble, you don't mean that. That's just fear talkin'."

Sarah gently took her husband's face between her hands, looked into his eyes and said, "Noble McAllister, you are a good man. An honest man. And in all the years we've been together, I have never known you to do anything but what was right — no matter what it cost you.

"Now I know this looks bad, and I surely don't know what the answer is or how it'll all come out. But here's what I do know, if we did what you're suggestin', that makes us no better than those murderers. And I don't think your conscience could live with that Noble. I know mine can't.

"What harm could there be in keepin' quiet about the boy for just a while longer? After all, whose gonna find out? Nobody ever comes out here, and I've already told Noah not to tell anyone about that baby yet, and he's a good boy, you know he won't tell.

"Besides, even when people do find out about him, no one ever has to know who he really belongs to.

"We can say he belongs, no, belonged, to my cousin's from Kentucky. We could say they ... died in a fire, or somethin' like that ... and since there's no other family, we took him in. Why would anybody question that?"

"Sound's like you got it all figured out. Except for the fact that you don't have family in Kentucky. Except for the fact that that boy is the spittin' image of his daddy. What about that? Huh?"

"Noble, you said yourself nobody knew anything about that Leonard and his wife. You said no one knew where they were stayin', or that they even had a child. For the short time they worked at the station there's probably only a few people who even saw 'em, and then only for a few minutes. I doubt there's anybody that could look at that boy and make the connection between him and that man ..."

"I did!" Noble interrupted.

"Yes, but you already knew who he belonged to — no one else does.

"As far as not havin' family in Kentucky, well, nobody knows that. We're not like most folks around here who've lived and died in this town for generations. In the ten years we've been here I don't think I've ever mentioned to anyone that I don't have family to speak of. So who would question our story?" Sarah continued coaxingly.

"I know it's a sin to lie Noble, but under the circumstance, I'm certain the good Lord will forgive us."

"Sarah, the fact that we've only been here for ten years is exactly why people are gonna be suspicious — we're outsiders to them. All it's gonna take is for one person to get a little curious, then do a little checkin', and then I'm done for.

"Who would believe I'm innocent when they find out we've been hidin' that little boy all this time? I know it ain't right to dump that kid off like his people did. But we have to do it Sarah, otherwise I could go to jail, or maybe even worse — I could even get the electric chair!

"How can I prove I didn't have anything to do with murderin' the Petersons?" Noble finished angrily.

Sarah closed her eyes. Releasing a long, slow sigh, she said, "Please Noble, don't do this."

Noble, teeth clenched tightly, glared at her.

"So you'd see me go to the electric chair to save that boy?" He spat, more as a statement than a question.

"Oh, Noble! That's not what I ..."

Noble couldn't bear to hear anymore. At that moment, he felt utterly betrayed by his own wife. He jumped up from the sofa and stormed out of the house, slamming the door soundly behind him.

Sarah put her hands to her face and began to cry, then after a time she got down on her knees. With folded hands and bowed head, she prayed like she had never prayed before.

She began by reciting one of her favorite passages from the Bible, the 23rd Psalm. "The Lord is my shepherd, I shall not want ..."

Then she continued on with a prayer for the souls of the recently departed. Then asked for forgiveness for everyone involved.

Finally, she prayed for her husband. She prayed that he would come to his senses, and realize how wrong it was to dump the boy off like his own family had.

Lastly, she prayed for God to give her and Noble the strength to deal with whatever was to come, knowing in her heart the ordeal was far from over. Before she rose to her feet, she whispered one final plea, "Father please let those men from Atlanta just pack up and go on home and leave us to tend to our own business. Amen."

Courage is not the lack of fear.
It is acting in spite of it.

— Mark Twain

Chapter Four

September 4th, 1959

Sarah swept a wisp of graying hair from her face as she stood over the stove scrambling eggs for Noah and Tommy's breakfast. After much consideration, they had chosen to call the drifter's boy, Tommy, after Sarah's great grandfather.

Her hair, almost all gray now, though she was only thirty-eight, was damp with sweat and clung annoyingly to her cheeks. Last night's thunderstorm had caused the humidity to skyrocket on this oppressively hot Monday morning, and she would have to wash up again before she took Tommy in for his first day of school.

Her heart pounded painfully at the thought. She should have enrolled him in school last year, but she hadn't because she was afraid Noble may have been right. Afraid that maybe someone would finally start poking around and find out who Tommy really was — the little boy Noah had found on the side of the road. The boy who belonged to those dead drifters. And she was terrified that the past was finally about to catch up with them.

Her prayer had been answered that night five years ago, and somehow the men from Dawson, including Noble, had managed to come through the ordeal practically unscathed.

The investigators from Atlanta had talked to nearly everyone in town before it was all over. And the men involved in murdering Leonard and his wife, held firmly to the story they had concocted about looking for, but never finding the two.

In the end, the men from Atlanta had gone off on a merry goose chase to find two transients, who even to this day were rotting away in unmarked graves out near Butcher Road.

Still, the tragedy had taken its toll, and had changed the people of Dawson forever. They were less friendly than before, and more distrustful and suspicious of newcomers, especially those just passing through.

Guilt weighed heavily on the men responsible for the death of the drifters, though they never spoke of it, they couldn't pass one another on the street without being reminded of what they had done.

Noble and Ernest had become bitter enemies, and though Ernest had denied it, Noble was convinced he had tried to set him up to take the fall for the Peterson murders if their story about the drifters had been challenged.

But the heaviest toll of all, at least in Sarah's mind, was the toll the tragedies had taken on her family.

Not for the first time, she wondered how differently things might have turned out, if the truth — the whole truth had come out five years ago.

At the time, the people of Dawson had been too caught up in the Peterson murders to be concerned about the boy the McAllisters had taken in. Like Sarah had predicted, no one questioned her story about why they had him or where he came from.

Now she couldn't help but worry that today someone would finally question his lineage, and it would be the beginning of their day of reckoning.

She scraped the eggs onto plates and called out, "Boys your breakfast is ready, hurry up before it gets cold."

The two came bouncing into the kitchen, Noah was filling Tommy in on what he could expect on his first day of school.

"Miss Lewis 'ill be your teacher, she's real nice Tommy, you'll like her a lot. Remember what I told ya, if anybody gives you any trouble, you just come to me, I'll fix it."

Despite her mood, Sarah had to smile at that. Tommy, who was quite small for his age, looked at Noah, and, hanging on his every word, nodded seriously.

The two were inseparable, and Noah had, out of necessity, become the younger boy's protector, especially whenever Noble was around.

Tommy looked around him, "Where's Pap, Momma?"

"He's out workin' in the shed," Sarah said, as a familiar twinge of pity enveloped her.

Tommy never dared call Noble "Pap" to his face. In fact, whenever Noble was around, he never called him anything, the two hardly spoke.

The first time he'd called Noble "Pap," Noble had screamed at him, "Don't call me that boy, I ain't your Pap!"

Tommy had burst into tears. That's when Sarah sat him down, though he was still very young, and explained the story of how they had taken him in after his parents had died in a fire. And from then on she tried to keep Tommy out of Noble's way whenever possible.

Noble had changed toward his own son too. Though he wasn't physically abusive, it seemed he was always yelling at him for something. Yet somehow, Noah seemed to take it in stride.

"Noah you wanna ride to school with Tommy and me this mornin'?"

"Naw, Curtis will be waitin' for me on the bus. Is Tommy gonna ride the bus home Momma?"

Sarah thought for a moment, not knowing how this day would turn out, she replied, "Oh I don't think so. Since it's his first day and all, I think I'll just pick him up. You wanna ride home with us?"

"No thanks, I'll get the bus," Noah said as he gulped down the last bite of eggs and headed for the door.

"C'mon Tommy, we better get goin' too. You wouldn't wanna be late for your first day of school now," she said nervously.

A short time later, Sarah sat in Vernon Watts' office with her heart, metaphorically in her throat. Vernon, the principal at Dawson Elementary, was a kindhearted man in his late fifties, and nearing retirement. He had been one of the few men in Dawson not involved in the dirty business of five years ago.

He was telling Sarah what a good boy her Noah was.

"... and smart too. You should be very proud of him Mrs. McAllister. I have a good feeling about that boy, he has a good head on his shoulder's."

"Indeed, he's going to go far."

"Thank you Mr. Watts, that's so nice to hear. I hope you find his brother, Tommy ... well, I'm sure you know they're not really brothers ... anyway, I hope he's the same way." Sarah stammered nervously.

"Yes, as I recall his parents died in ... what was it? A fire?"

Sarah's mouth became so dry, she could hardly speak.

"Uh, yeah, it was a fire."

"I believe his father was your brother?"

"No, no, I don't have a brother ... he was my cousin ... from Kentucky ... once removed," she continued to embellish.

"That's right, now I remember. Poor thing, it must have been really hard on him, being so young and all. So what were their names?"

Sarah felt her knees go weak, and was certain she was on the verge of fainting.

"Well, that would be ... WWWilkinson ... uh, Tom and Rita Wilkinson," she quickly made up the names.

"But you see Mr. Watts, Tommy goes by our last name. We figured it would be easier that way. Since ... there's no birth record ... and ... nothin' legal with his name on it ... because well, you see they had him at home ... they were kind of backward that way ... they moved around a lot ... and everything they had, burned in the, the fire ... and ..." Sarah felt as though she couldn't shut up as she continued with one halting explanation after another, which seemed to require another, then another and on an on she went until finally, Vernon Watts saved her from herself.

"It's okay Mrs. McAllister, I get the picture, and I can see it's still difficult for you to talk about. We'll just enroll him as a McAllister."

Sarah was so relieved he did not require further information, that she couldn't stop thanking him as he gently ushered her out of his office.

Noble came out of his workshed when he heard Sarah pull into the driveway.

"So what happened with Mr. Watts?" he asked nonchalantly.

Though he tried not to show it, she knew he'd been worrying about this day as well.

"It's okay Noble, I didn't have any trouble enrollin' Tommy for school."

Without another word, Noble turned around and went back to his shed. Sarah watched him walk away with a heavy ache in her heart.

It wasn't even nine o'clock and she could already smell the liquor on his breath. That's how it was more often than not these days.

The ordeal of five years ago had nearly destroyed Noble, or more accurately, it was destroying him still. And he had never forgiven her for what he considered her betrayal.

Sadly, he was so consumed by hate and anger, there was no room left in his heart for anything else, and the only way he could alleviate the pain was with a bottle. Despite her efforts, Sarah could not find a way to reach him, a way to help him forgive them all and move on.

A bully is not reasonable —
he is persuaded only by threats.

— Marie De France

Chapter Five

Three o'clock came and went unnoticed by Sarah, in fact, she had been so busy around the farm, she'd lost all track of time. It wasn't until she saw Noah walking up the driveway that she realized school had been out for half an hour already.

She jumped in the pick-up, started the engine and called for Noah to climb in.

"Did you see Tommy after school son? Did you see him waitin' for me?" Sarah asked, the worry clear in her voice.

"No, I only saw him once today, at recess."

"Oh Lord, he's gonna be scared to death waitin' there all alone," she said, half to herself.

A short time later they pulled into the school yard, got out of the pick-up and looked around, but there was no sign of Tommy.

Sarah was about to go inside and ask if anyone had seen him, when Noah called out, "Hang on Momma, I think I see him."

Pointing toward a little boy, he continued, "Over there, I think that's him."

They jumped back into the truck and started down the road. Tommy was walking in the opposite direction of the farm, his head hung low as he shuffled along slowly. Sarah and Noah pulled up beside him and Noah called his name. Tommy stopped but didn't look up.

Noah jumped out and took his hand, "C'mon Li'l Bit, you're headin' the wrong way," he said affectionately.

When Tommy lifted his head, Noah felt an instant sting of anger. Tommy's face was puffy and red, he was bleeding from his nose and his bottom lip.

"What the sam hell happened to you?" Noah hissed.

Sarah sucked in her breath loudly, "Noah McAllister! You watch your mouth little man!" She said before she saw what caused his outburst.

When she did, she couldn't help herself, she also blurted out, "What the sam hell happened Tommy?"

Tommy shrugged his shoulders noncommittally, then silently shuffled behind Noah to the truck. When Sarah asked the question again, he threw his hands to his face and burst into tears.

"Some boys just started pushin' and shovin' me. When I falled, one of 'em got on top of me and started sockin' me in the face. I don't know why they did it, I didn't do nothin' to 'em."

"It's okay son, it's gonna be all right," Sarah said consolingly.

Seething with fury, Noah told himself he would find whoever did this to Tommy and teach them a lesson they'd never forget!

When they got home, Sarah and Noah rushed Tommy to the bathroom and began to clean his swollen, bloody face.

Noble heard the truck come to a screeching halt in the driveway and came out of his shed to see what was going on. He watched Sarah and Noah shuffle Tommy into the house. After a moment or two, he followed them inside.

"What happened?" He asked as he looked over Sarah's shoulder at Tommy.

Sarah turned to him with tears in her eyes, as she gently washed his face she said, "Some boys at school beat him up."

Noble shrugged his shoulders, "Figures," he said, then turned and headed for the front door.

A red haze of rage engulfed Sarah. She handed the washcloth to Noah, spun around and ran after him.

"Noble McAllister how can you say such a thing? You don't even know what happened!"

"I don't need to know Sarah. That boy's been trouble from the moment I laid eyes on him, and he's gonna be trouble 'til the last time I lay eyes on him!" Noble bellowed as he stormed out of the house.

Sometimes Sarah hated her husband, sometimes she hated him so much she wanted to strike him ... before that thought could fully articulate in her mind, she whispered a prayer.

"Lord you know I don't mean that. But I swear, sometimes, sometimes it's just so hard to love that man when he's so filled up with pity for himself he can't see what he's doin' to the people who love him still."

Then she turned back to the boys. By the look on their faces, she knew they had heard every word spoken between Noble and herself. It pained her greatly to see the heartache Noble's remarks had caused Tommy, which showed clearly in his eyes.

Noah's eyes on the other hand were filled with something else, something that chilled Sarah to the bone. Her strapping eleven-year-old was staring past her, toward the shed, his eyes filled with murderous rage.

Without looking at his mother, Noah handed the washcloth back to her and started for the door.

Sarah grabbed him by the arm and said, "Where you goin' son?"

"To talk to Pap," he stated determinedly.

Sarah released his arm and sighed, she could only handle one crisis at a time, and right now, Tommy's seemed the most urgent.

She sat him down in a chair and said, "You wanna tell me what happened now?"

Tommy hung his head, and began softly, "I 'ready told you Momma. I was waitin' for you like you said, but you didn't come, so I went over to the swings. I was just swingin', then some boys come up and one of 'em grabs my swing and he says, 'Hey boy, what's your name?' I said Tommy.

"Then he grabs my shirt and says, 'Look fellas, look at this here ugly old shirt Tommy's wearin'. What's the matter, ain't your people got no money to buy you good clothes?' I says, 'I don't know,' then he starts pushin' me, and them other boys start pushin' me too. Then I falled and that big boy sits on me and starts sockin' me in the face.

"Then one of them other boy's says, 'Come on Tipton, 'fore the principal catches us.' Then they just left Momma, that's all." Tommy finished in a whisper.

Sarah shook her head, turned her eyes toward heaven and sighed heavily. Of all the children in Dawson, why on earth did Ernest Tipton's son Billy have to be involved? she wondered.

Billy Tipton was a big, heavyset boy, who looked like he was always frowning because of the excessive weight on his fleshy face.

He was the same age as Noah, but had been held back a year, so was only in the fourth grade.

"Well, we'll go talk to Mr. Watts tomorrow Tommy. We'll see to it those boys get punished."

Fear leapt into Tommy's eyes and he said, "No Momma, you can't! Then them boys 'ill really get me for tellin' on 'em!"

"Tommy, you can't let those boys get away with somethin' like this, or else they'll never leave you alone."

"Yes they will Momma, Noah said so." Tommy replied confidently.

Noah walked purposefully out to his father's workshed, without knocking he yanked the door open and shouted, "Why'd you say those things back there Pap? Why'd you hurt Tommy like that? What'd he ever do to you?"

Noble stood dumbfounded for a moment. Noah had never raised his voice or spoken with such disrespect before.

Finally, Noble ground out, "Who the sam hell you talkin' to boy? I suggest you watch your mouth before I take a strap to your backside!" and then, "And anyway, you don't know what that trouble-makin' little runt has done to me, so just stay out of it!"

Years later, Noah would look back on this moment and not be able to recall what happened next. One minute he was standing there, the next thing he knew, his mother was pulling him and his father apart.

Sarah and Tommy came flying out of the house when they heard Noble bellowing loud enough to wake the dead. Sarah jumped from the porch and dashed across the yard to the shed.

When she yanked the door open and saw Noah pummeling his father with his fists as they rolled around on the floor, she nearly fainted.

Although Noah was a big, strong boy, he was no match for his father. And had Noble been inclined, he could have felled his son with one powerful blow from his hand. But to his credit, he simply threw his hands up to protect his face and let Noah have at him.

"Lord Almighty! Stop it! Stop it right now!" Sarah screamed at them.

Neither was listening, and the ruckus continued until she finally grabbed her son around the waist and pulled him with all her might.

The unexpected jolt caused Noah to fall backward directly on top of her.

Sarah hit the ground with a loud "whoosh," as the air was violently torn from her lungs.

When she was able to catch her breath, she glared at her husband and son, who were now staring at her with guilt-ridden expressions.

"Noah, you get yourself back to the house right now!" Sarah snapped without taking her eyes off the two as she stood up and dusted herself off.

Noah quickly, quietly, obeyed.

Before Sarah could completely collect herself, Noble grinned, then he began to chuckle, and then his chuckle turned into full-out, belly-busting laughter.

Sarah was so caught off guard, she began to laugh right along with him, momentarily forgetting the seriousness of the situation. Pretty soon they were both laughing so hard tears were streaming down their faces.

When the laughter died down, Noble gingerly rubbed his chin where Noah had managed to clip him before he threw up his hands to protect his face.

"Sarah, that boy of ours walloped me good. I think he dang near broke my jaw."

"What happened Noble?" Sarah asked, turning serious again.

"Well, Noah comes out here screamin' somethin' about the way I treat that boy in there, and how it ain't right. Then before I know it, he's tryin' to beat the life out of me. Then you came out and, that was the end of it."

"Hmm. Noah's a good boy isn't he Noble?' Sarah replied pensively.

"Yeah, I guess so."

"You know somethin' else? Tommy's a good boy too. And if you'd give him half a chance, you'd see that. I don't think you know how much they both love you. I don't think you know how your meanness toward that little boy hurts 'em both. Cuz if you did, I have to believe you wouldn't do it."

Noble snorted in disgust, "Sarah, you go on and believe whatever makes you feel better. But I don't care one bit about that boy. And I'm never goin' to!

"Now we may have dodged a bullet today with that principal. But someday Sarah, it's all gonna catch up to us — you wait and see. Then let's see how you feel about him.

"You'll feel just like me! Now go on and get out of here, I've got work to do," he finished gruffly, then turned away from her.

Sarah stared at him sadly. For one brief moment, she almost believed ... no, she couldn't bear to finish the thought.

"Noble McAllister, I will never feel like you. I will never be so filled up with hate and self-pity that I blame all the bad things in my life on an innocent little boy.

"You might be right about the truth catchin' up with us someday. But even then I won't blame Tommy. He didn't have anything to do with those murders, and he never asked to be dumped off like he was no better than a piece of garbage. It's just the way it happened. There's nothin' else we can do but get over it and move on."

"That's easy for you to say, Sarah, but I don't see it that way!" Noble spat back at her.

Sarah didn't bother responding, she just turned around and left the shed.

Noah saw his mother coming across the yard and met her at the front door.

"Momma, are you all right? I didn't mean to hurt you," he said with great concern.

"I'm fine Noah. You didn't hurt me. Why don't you come on out here and sit on the porch with me a minute, we'll have a little talk." Sarah said.

Noah shrugged his shoulders and followed his mother to the front porch step, then sat down beside her.

"Noah, you know what you did to your Pap just now was wrong, don't ya?"

"Why does he hate Tommy so much Momma?"

"Son, it's an awful long story, and it's not that he hates him ..." Sarah lied.

"No Momma, you're wrong! He does hate him!" Noah interrupted.

"Sometimes I see him lookin' at Tommy when he thinks no one's watchin', and I get scared, cuz I think maybe he's gonna do somethin' to Tommy, somethin' bad."

"Noah, don't talk like that! Your Pap would never hurt either one of you." Sarah admonished, though secretly, she wasn't so sure.

"Now listen to me, when your Pap comes in for supper, I want you to apologize for what you did, you hear me?"

"No! I'm not gonna do it Momma, cuz I'm not sorry for what I did. He had it comin'!"

"Noah McAllister, you'll do like I told you, or you'll go to bed without your supper!" Sarah snapped angrily.

Noah went to bed hungry.

Later that night Tommy crept quietly to Noah's bed.

"Noah, wake up, I brought you a piece of chicken," he whispered softly.

Noah turned over and smiled gratefully. After he devoured the tasty morsel, he whispered, "Who was it that beat you up today?" though he already had a pretty good idea who it was.

When Tommy confirmed his suspicion, Noah shook his head, "Yeah, that's what I thought."

"Tommy, don't worry about those boys, I'll take care of 'em tomorrow okay?"

"Okay Noah."

"Tommy, I'd never let anything really bad happen to you ... you know that right?"

"Yeah, I know," Tommy whispered back, trusting in Noah's words with all his heart.

Difficulties are meant to rouse, not discourage.
The human spirit is to grow by conflict.

— William Ellery Channing

Chapter Six

Sarah scraped an extra helping of eggs onto Noah's plate. Although she felt bad about sending him to bed hungry the night before, she knew the punishment was justified. God only knew what would happen the next time he decided to light into his father like that. Maybe the next time Noble would be too liquored up to care about what he did to his son. That thought sent a shiver down Sarah's spine, because she had stayed awake all night with that on her mind.

"Momma, I might be late comin' home from school today," Noah said, interrupting his mother's private musing.

"How come?"

"Well, I might stay after to help Miss Baker clean erasers," Noah lied.

"Oh, okay. I was gonna go talk to Mr. Watts about what those boys did to Tommy yesterday, so I'll just wait for ya, and give you a ride home."

"No!" Both boys nearly shouted at the same time.

Sarah looked at them suspiciously, "All right, what's goin' on?"

"If you do that, Tommy'll get beat up again for sure! You don't know Billy Tipton and his buddies. They like to pick on the little kids, and if any of 'em tell on him, they'll really get it! So Momma please, just let me talk to 'em. They won't bother Tommy again, I promise," Noah finished solemnly.

Sarah thought about it, then said, "Noah, if that's what those boys are doin', a grown-up needs to step in and stop 'em before they really hurt one of those little ones."

"Momma, it won't do any good. Please, let me just talk to 'em today. If they bother Tommy again, then you can tell Mr. Watts."

After some consideration, and against her better judgement, Sarah agreed, though she warned, "Noah listen to me, I don't want any fightin'. You just tell 'em to leave Tommy alone, then we'll leave it at that and see what happens. You hear me?"

Noah nodded, and said, "Thanks Momma."

Sarah looked at Tommy, aside from a slight cut on his lip, he looked none the worse for wear.

She tousled his hair and said, "You gonna be okay Li'l Bit?"

"Yeah," he replied with a smile.

"C'mon Tommy we better get goin' before we miss the bus."

On the ride to school, Noah told his best friend Curtis, what Billy and his buddies had done, and what he planned to do about it.

"Boy, Noah, I sure wish I could be there when you give that Tipton what for! He's had it comin' for a long time. You sure you don't want me to come along?"

"Naw, just make sure Tommy gets on the bus after school okay?"

"You got it."

When the last bell of the day rang, Noah glanced at Curtis and nodded. Curtis was the first in line to leave the room, while Noah shuffled books around in his desk, pretending to look for something, so he could lag behind the others and get lost among the sea of children.

Since Tipton lived fairly close to school he never rode the bus, nor did his cohorts. And today, luck was on Noah's side, because Billy and his buddies were taking the longer, less crowded way home, down a dirt path near the creek.

A further stroke of luck was that Noah managed to get ahead of them and conceal himself in between some bushes without anyone's notice.

He allowed the boys, who at that very moment were joking and laughing about what they had done to Tommy, to pass in front of him. Then he stepped out from the overgrown shrubbery and shouted, "Hey Tipton!"

All four stopped and spun around to look at Noah.

Billy Tipton was as tall as Noah but outweighed him by at least thirty pounds. The other three, a year younger than the two bigger boys, were of average size.

"Yeah?" Billy sneered.

"You know that little kid you beat up yesterday?"

"Yeah, what of it?" Billy continued arrogantly, almost proudly.

"That kid was my brother, Tommy."

"So," Billy answered, a little less bravely.

"So? So I wonder how you're gonna feel when I beat the piss outta you?" Noah spewed, feeling his anger rise at Tipton's total lack of remorse.

The other boys could sense Billy's growing fear, and while it was one thing to go around beating up smaller kids on the playground, this was a fifth grader — a big fifth grader! And none of the younger boys wanted to tangle with him.

In unspoken unison the three took a step back from Tipton. Then they turned on their heels and took off running.

Billy, left standing alone, felt an uncomfortable tingling of alarm way down in the pit of his stomach. It was one thing to mouth off when you knew you outnumbered your adversary, and quite another when the odds were less stacked in your favor.

"Listen McAllister, we were just funnin' with him, we didn't really mean to hurt him," Tipton said cajolingly, attempting to weasel his way out of what he suspected was going to be a pretty painful thumping.

Billy's words fell on deaf ears, and seeing no other way out, he turned to run. Unfortunately, he was neither as light nor agile as his cowardly companions, and Noah caught up with him in a few short strides.

Noah grabbed him by the cuff of his collar and spun him around. Then he pulled his right arm back as far as it would go, and let fly with a punch to Tipton's jaw that nearly knocked him off his feet.

Billy swung at Noah blindly, but the blow barely glanced his shoulder.

Noah hit him again with his left fist causing Billy to stagger backward. Pretty soon he was pummeling Tipton with both fists until he knocked him to the ground.

Finally, Noah looked down into Billy's bloody face and said, "Don't ever come near my brother again Tipton, or you'll be sorry!"

Then snorting in disgust, Noah stood up, turned from the pathetic boy and walked away.

As Billy lay on the ground wiping the sweat, dirt, and blood from his face, he felt warm, wet liquid trickle down his legs as his treacherous bladder released its contents.

"Ahhhh, shoot!" Billy hissed half under his breath. Then he began to cry like a baby as he pushed himself up, got to his feet and ran home.

From the kitchen Sarah heard the screen door open, and called out, "Noah is that you?"

"Yeah Momma, it's me," he said, quickly heading for the bedroom to change his clothes before his mother saw Billy's blood on his shirt.

Too late. She came out of the kitchen before he had taken more than two steps.

"Noah McAllister, I thought I told you no fightin'!" Sarah said angrily.

"Momma, he had it comin'! He wasn't even sorry for what he did to Tommy." Noah responded steadily.

Deep down, Sarah whole-heartedly agreed that the Tipton boy had it coming. Yet regardless of her private opinion, she was determined to make Noah understand that fighting was never the answer and usually caused more problems than it solved.

However, before she could begin that lecture, Ernest's squad car came barreling to a screeching halt in front of the McAllister house.

Before Sarah could even reach the front door, Ernest was out of the car bellowing.

"Noble McAllister, get your raggedy butt out here now!"

Sarah looked at Noah and Tommy and said, "You two stay in here," then she bravely walked out to face Tipton.

Noble came out of the shed and both McAllisters met the Tiptons in the front yard. Ernest grabbed his son by the neck and shook him.

"Look here! Look here what your boy done to my Billy!" he shouted.

Billy's left eye was swollen nearly shut and already turning black and blue. His lip was split in two places and though Sarah couldn't be sure, she thought his nose looked a bit disjointed.

She crossed her arms defiantly in front of her, "Sheriff Tipton, why don't you ask your boy here what him and his friends did to my Tommy yesterday."

Glancing sideways at his wife, Noble said calmly, "Sarah, go on back to the house. I'll take care of this."

Reluctantly, Sarah turned around and walked very slowly to the porch.

"Now come on Noble, you know this ain't right. You gotta do somethin' about this!"

Noble, savoring the moment, grinned broadly and said, "Oh, I don't know Ernest, looks to me like junior here got what he deserved."

Tipton's face turned purple with righteous indignation, he stammered and stuttered for several seconds, then finally choked out, "If you ain't gonna do nothin' about it, I'll just arrest the little son of a gun!"

Sarah came flying off the porch at the same time Noble grabbed Ernest by the collar, and yanked him in close.

Gritting his teeth, Noble hissed, "Oh just try it! I really want you to. Cuz I've been waitin' a long time for a reason to pound your sorry butt into the ground!"

Fear leapt into Ernest's eyes as he desperately tried to pull away. After several moments Noble released him. Tipton quickly stepped back out of reach, gasping for air.

When he collected himself, he said, "One of these days we're gonna settle up McAllister."

Noble opened his arms wide in invitation, "I'm ready when you are and lookin' forward to it. Oh, but Ernest, it might be a good idea to leave your gun at home. We both know what happens when you get nervous. We both know how that gun of yours tends to go off on accident."

Now Ernest's face turned a mottled shade of grey. He opened his mouth to speak, but nothing came out, and before he could form the words, his son blurted out, "Hey! You can't talk to my dad like that!"

Ernest looked at Billy angrily, then slapped him on the back of the head and said, "Shut up stupid and get in the car."

"But Daaaaad," Billy whined.

"I said get in the car!" Tipton shouted.

Before Ernest joined his son, he looked across the hood of the squad car at Noble and said just loud enough for the other man to hear, "Let the past die Noble, everyone else has. Hell, look at you man — you've let this thing eat away at you 'till it's turned you into nothin' more than the town drunk! Get over it before it completely ruins your life."

Ernest was in the car and backing down the dirt driveway before Noble had a chance to respond.

Just above a whisper Noble remarked morosely, "Yeah you rat bastard, that's easy for you to say, you don't have to look at that dead man's face every single day!" referring to Tommy's uncanny resemblance to his father.

"You're not the one that's gonna get the electric chair when the crap hits the fan either!"

Through the years as Noble's mind became foggier and foggier from drink, he had convinced himself that someday one of two things would happen — someone was going to find out who Tommy really was and draw the obvious conclusion, at least in Noble's besotted mind, that he had been in cahoots with those murdering drifters. And as payback for the Petersons, the townspeople would do everything they could to see to it that he got the electric chair.

The other scenario, and the one which haunted Noble's alcohol-induced dreams nearly every night, was where Tommy would turn on them, just as his parents had turned on the Petersons.

In Noble's recurring nightmare, he would find himself at the front door of the Peterson home, only in the dream it was his and Sarah's house. He never wanted to go in, yet he was compelled to. Once he stepped inside, an exact reenactment of what had taken place in real life played itself out, except instead of finding the pulverized bodies of Harvey and Edna, it was Sarah and him.

That's where the nightmare would end and Noble would, more often than not, wake up in a cold sweat with a scream lodged in his throat.

"Noble? ... Noble?" Sarah had to repeat herself before he acknowledged her presence.

Noble mentally shook himself to clear the horrific images from his head, then said gruffly, "What?"

"You all right?"

"Why Sarah? What're you gonna do about it if I'm not?" Noble threw at her viciously.

His words cut straight to her heart, as tears sprang to her eyes she looked at her husband with a pained expression and replied softly, "Whatever I can."

Noble made a noise that sounded like a cross between a chuckle and a snort.

"Well, you're just about a day late and a dollar short Sarah." And then, "I'm fine! Just go on back to the house."

Noble turned away and walked back to his shed, leaving Sarah to stare after him in silence.

From the front window, Tommy and Noah had witnessed the whole thing. And when Tommy saw Billy's face, he looked up at Noah in awe and admiration and said, "Gee Noah, you really gived him what for."

To which Noah replied, "I told you Li'l Bit, nobody's ever gonna hurt you and get away with it as long as I'm around."

When Sarah walked back into the house, both Tommy and Noah looked at her expectantly.

"We'll talk about this later. Now go on and get cleaned up," Sarah said, then went into the kitchen to finish making supper.

Later that night in bed, Sarah said, "Noble?"

"Yeah?"

"Maybe Ernest has a point. Maybe ..."

"Ahhh, Jesus, Joseph, and Mary!" Noble hissed, jumping up from the bed in one fluid movement.

"Noble, I just meant ..."

"Don't say another word! Not another word woman!" Noble ground out as he yanked his pants on. Then he grabbed his shirt from the back of the chair and stormed, barefoot out of the house.

Noble marched angrily across the yard and to his shed. Throwing the door open wide he stepped to the middle of the room and pulled the string hanging from the ceiling. Harsh, white light flooded the space from the single light bulb hanging from the rafter.

He looked around for several seconds, when he didn't find what he was looking for, he began frantically pulling out drawers and turning them upside down, spilling the contents onto the ground. Finally he found it, a nearly full bottle of whiskey.

Noble quickly unscrewed the cap, put his mouth over the opening and turned the bottle upside down allowing the warm, burning liquid to slide smoothly down his throat. After a few seconds, he set the bottle aside and wiped his mouth with the back of his hand.

How dare Sarah side with that lowlife! How could she be so disloyal? She was his wife damn it! And as her husband she should take his side no matter what! Noble's mind raged.

He tipped the bottle up again and took another long, loud, gulping swig.

Yeah, maybe if Sarah had been a more loyal wife, maybe today his life would be worth more than a plugged nickel. Maybe if she had listened to him and gotten rid of that little wart all those years ago, maybe he could've moved past the tragedies like everyone else seemed to have.

And maybe, just maybe, if Noah had never brought that worthless little toad home in the first place, he would never have been involved in any of it!

Noble glanced toward the house, as though he could see it through the windowless wall. Smoldering hate filled his eyes, as the objects of his loathing lay sleeping soundly, completely oblivious to the hostility they provoked in the elder McAllister. Except one — she was down on her knees praying for a husband's heart to open up and forgive them all.

Noble threw his head back and downed the last of the whisky without taking a breath, then impulsively threw it angrily against the wall, shattering the bottle into a thousand pieces.

Do not fear death so much,
but rather the inadequate life.

— Bertolt Brecht

Chapter Seven

July 9th, 1963

Sarah kicked at the thin sheet in frustration. It was two o'clock in the morning and Noble was still out boozing she guessed. Noble's ritual of staying out all night, sleeping most the day away, then starting all over again, began four years ago, shortly after Noah had gotten into that fight with the Tipton boy.

Why she was more bothered by it tonight than any other night was a mystery to her. But whatever the reason, she was quickly working herself into a full-blown fury.

Finally, she jumped out of bed and walked over to the window and opened it as far as it would go. A cool, soothing breeze gently caressed her warm skin. Closing her eyes, she listened to the soft chirping of crickets outside, and felt the tension slowly ebb from her body.

Wrapping her arms around herself, Sarah realized why she was more bothered tonight by Noble's absence than usual. Tonight she would have welcomed his touch, in fact, she longed for it.

It wasn't often she would allow herself to think about the past, or what might have been if things had turned out differently. But she was in a melancholy mood and couldn't seem to stop her thoughts from wandering back to a time when things had been good between the two of them. A time when something as simple as a tender look from Noble caused her pulse to quicken in anticipation.

Tonight she would give anything to feel that again. Remembering how wonderful it felt once to be wrapped in his strong arms and enveloped in his love made her heart ache for what they'd lost.

These days, it wasn't often he came to their bed for any other reason than to sleep off a drunken stupor. And on those rare occasions when he wasn't too drunk to pass out, what passed between them was anything but loving.

At that moment, in Sarah's heart, she would have given anything, paid any price, to have the good man she had married back again.

A moment later the front door banged loudly, startling her out of her private thoughts. She quickly jumped back into bed. However, tonight she did not pretend sleep. Instead, she fluffed the pillows behind her head and tried to smooth her hair into place while she waited for Noble to join her.

She could hear him mumbling to himself as he stumbled around the living room. And it was hard to hold onto her desire of moments ago, but she tried.

It wasn't long before the house grew quiet again and she had to strain to listen for his footsteps. With a sinking feeling he had passed out somewhere beyond their bedroom, she got up and started for the door.

All of a sudden, it sounded as though hell was reigning down upon the McAllister household. Noble began to bellow, Tommy screamed, and Noah was shouting at his father to let go.

Bolting from the bed, Sarah raced to the boys bedroom where she found a crazed Noble holding Tommy above the bed shaking him by the throat like a rag doll.

Noah was pounding on his father with his fists. However, Noble seemed completely immune to the blows.

"You little worthless piece of garbage, it's all your fault! It's all your fault you little bastard! Your people were right to throw you away! You've been nothin' but trouble, you little wart!" Noble shouted.

For the span of a heartbeat Sarah stood rooted to the spot in terror. Then she leapt at her husband and grabbed hold of his arm, screaming, "Noble! Noble! Let go! You're gonna kill him! Please Noble! Please let him go!"

Still holding onto Tommy by the throat with one hand, Noble swung his free arm at his wife, knocking her to the ground.

Sarah scrambled backward out of the room, ran to the kitchen and grabbed a butcher's knife from the utensil drawer. Then she stumbled back to the bedroom and rushed at Noble with the knife drawn high above her head.

With all the strength she possessed, Sarah swung the knife in a downward motion, slicing deep into Noble's arm, between his shoulder and elbow. Though the wound was not all that serious, it bled profusely and carried enough of a sting to cause Noble to abruptly release Tommy, who dropped to the bed gasping for air. Then he turned to Sarah in disbelief. Before he could react further, she raised the knife again and pressed it to his heart.

"I will cut your heart out! I mean it! I'll cut your black heart right out if you touch either one of my babies again!" she screamed hysterically.

Clutching his bleeding arm, Noble backed a safe distance away from his panic-strickened wife and stared at her in astonishment.

Then a slow, menacing smile crept across Noble's haggard and hollow face.

"That's right mother hen, there's a fox loose in the chicken coop, better keep a real good eye on them li'l chickadees, cuz that crafty ol' fox is gonna get 'em. Yes sir, he's gonna get 'em! In the end, he sure is gonna get 'em!" Then he backed out of the bedroom, the sound of his own insane laughter trailing after him.

As soon as he was clear of the door, Sarah, still clutching the bloody knife, ran to it and locked it. When she turned back to the boys, and saw the same terror she felt mirrored in their faces, she dropped her weapon and hurried to comfort them.

Noah, just fifteen, looked at his mother with eyes that seemed to her as old as Solomon's. Shaking his head, he whispered softly, "Why Momma?"

Sarah didn't trust herself to speak, she simply shook her head and shrugged her shoulders. Then turned her attention to Tommy, whose neck was covered with angry red marks. His face was ghostly pale as he stared at her blankly.

Sarah thought he might be in shock. She shook him gently, and said softly, "Tommy. Son are you all right?"

It seemed an eternity passed before he responded. When he finally spoke, his eyes filled with tears. In a raspy voice he croaked, "I'm sorry Momma."

That Tommy should feel responsible for Noble's actions ignited a raging fire in Sarah's heart.

"Son, you don't have anything to be sorry for. None of this is your fault! You've never done anything to that darn fool, except try to love him!"

She had never spoken out so harshly against Noble to the boys, but she didn't regret it, because this time he had gone too far!

His indifference toward his own son and outright and obvious hatred of Tommy had not been enough to open her eyes. It hadn't been enough, when, thanks to his status as the town drunk, few people cared to do business with the McAllisters these days.

And the handful still willing to buy their chickens allowed them to do little more than eke out a meager existence. In fact, "poor" would have been a step up by Sarah's estimation. They were almost entirely alienated from the Dawson community, thanks to Noble. Still, that had not been enough to turn her heart completely against him.

But now, she realized for perhaps the first time, that there was nothing good or decent left in Noble McAllister. And so without remorse, though she was sure she would burn in hell for it later, she wished him dead.

Hugging the boys tightly to her, Sarah said, "Noah, I'm gonna get a cold rag for Tommy. I want you to lock this door behind me all right?"

Noah stared at her for a moment, then said steadily, "Let me go Momma."

Sarah could hardly choke back the tears, giving him a weak smile, she said, "No son, I'll go. It'll be all right I promise. Just don't open this door 'til you hear me call to you okay?"

Noah looked down at the knife Sarah had dropped, then back at his mother, swallowing hard, he said, "Momma, take the knife. I'll come runnin' if ..."

Sarah did not allow him to finish that sentence, "It'll be all right Noah, I promise," though she did pick up the butcher's knife before slipping from the room.

Standing in the dark hallway, she clutched the weapon tightly in both hands as she listened for any sound that Noble was still in the house.

When she was confident that he had either left, or had passed out, she crept quietly to the bathroom. Not daring to turn on a light, she fumbled blindly in the darkness until she found what she was looking for.

After wetting the washcloth, she turned toward the door and was startled to find Noble standing directly in front of her blocking her only exit.

Sarah jumped back in shock, dropping the butcher's knife which clattered noisily to the floor. For several tense moments they stared at one another in silence.

Noble's features, distorted by shadow, made him look even more menacing.

"I'm not gonna hurt you Sarah," he whispered, his speech slurred from the alcohol.

"I'd never hurt you, you know that right?"

Suddenly, her fear evaporated.

"Noble, for nearly ten long years now, you've done nothin' else but hurt me. And not only me, but you've hurt our son too, a good son who loved you with all his heart. You've also hurt an innocent little boy who never wanted anything from you but love and acceptance. A little boy who, despite your hatefulness and meanness toward him, would have forgiven you for every bad thing you've done to him, if you'd shown him even the smallest kindness.

You know until tonight, I actually believed there was somethin' good left inside of you. But the truth of it is, there's not. And now I'm just sorry that it took you nearly killin' my Tommy for me to see it. But I do finally see it. In fact, I think we'd all be better off if you were ... if you were ... gone."

"You mean dead don't you Sarah?"

"No, I mean gone ... just gone."

Tears sprang to Noble's eyes, he wiped at them furiously but couldn't control the muffled sob that escaped him.

Once he regained control of himself, he said emotionally, "Why's my life so bad Sarah? I don't deserve this hell on earth!"

"Where do you think the rest of us have been Noble? — sufferin' right along with you, that's where!

"I know you think that all your problems would have been solved if only you had gotten rid of Tommy like you wanted to all those years ago. But if you had dumped Tommy off like you wanted to, could you have lived with yourself? Could you really have done that to an innocent baby?"

In weariness Sarah finished, "What happened was a tragedy for everyone. But we handled it the best we could Noble. I don't know why you've allowed such hate to replace every good and decent thing that was in you.

"Don't forget, you're the one that tried to save Miss Edna. You're the one that tried to stop those men from killin' Tommy's daddy.

"In my book that makes you a hero. The only real man there that day. That's right — you were once a man to be admired Noble, now you're just a drunk to be pitied."

With that, Sarah pushed past her husband and walked with purposeful steps back to the bedroom.

For several moments Noble stood rooted to the spot as Sarah's parting words fell heavily on his heart. Then he quietly left the house, knowing what he had to do.

Sarah knocked softly on the door and called out, "It's me Noah."
Noah opened the door cautiously and said, "Is he gone Momma?"
"Yeah, it's okay son."

After applying the cool compress to Tommy's throat, Sarah crawled into bed beside him and gently ran her fingers through his thick black hair until he fell asleep.

Just before she drifted off to sleep herself, Noah whispered from his bed across the room, "Momma, this is never gonna end is it?"

Sarah waited a long time before answering, in a voice thick with sadness, she said, "I don't know Noah," after several more moments, she continued, "I wish I had a better answer son, but I don't."

*Remember this — that there is a proper dignity and proportion
to be observed in the performance of every act of life.*

— Marcus Aurelius Antoninus

Chapter Eight

The next morning Sarah woke with a start. Tommy was still sleeping peacefully beside her, but when she looked across the room, Noah's bed was empty.

Raw fear, unlike anything she had ever known propelled her out of bed.

Running out into the hallway, she called, "Noah?"

After racing through the house and checking every room, with still no sign of her son, Sarah was on the verge of hysteria. In her nightgown and bare feet, she ran outside screaming for Noah to answer her.

When nothing but the stillness of the morning greeted her, Sarah rushed toward the shed as though a life depended on it.

As she breathlessly threw open the door, her immediate reaction was a gasp of horror. Then her legs buckled beneath her and she collapsed to the floor.

"Dear God in heaven Noah, what have you done? What have you done?" she screamed.

Time seemed to stand still as Sarah sat sprawled on the floor, her eyes riveted on the bloated, purple, unrecognizable face of her husband.

When she felt a hand gently squeeze her shoulder, she jumped like a scared rabbit and scooted across the floor.

"Momma, c'mon, let me take you out of here. C'mon," Noah tried coaxingly.

To Sarah, Noah looked almost as frightening as Noble. The entire left side of his face was swollen and already beginning to show signs of an ugly, black and blue bruise, and his eyes were so red they almost appeared to be bleeding.

"What have you done? What in God's name have you done Noah?" Sarah whispered weakly.

Noah didn't flinch from the question or from his mother's penetrating stare. Reaching out to her, he said evenly, "C'mon Momma, let me take you out of here, then I'll tell you what happened. Please."

At first Sarah resisted, but eventually she allowed herself to be led from the shed, though she had to lean heavily on Noah for support.

Once they were inside, Noah led her to the sofa, then knelt in front of her.

Taking her hands into his, he said, "Momma, last night I stayed awake for a long time thinkin' about what Pap said — that in the end he was gonna get us. 'Member that Momma? 'Member him sayin' that last night?

"Well, I figured he meant it. I figured he wouldn't stop comin' after Tommy 'til he finally did kill him. And I couldn't let that happen.

"I figured I had to at least try and stop him once and for all. So after you and Tommy went to sleep, I went out to find Pap."

Noah momentarily hesitated, hung his head and took a deep breath, then looked up at Sarah. With tears shimmering in his eyes he continued, "When I went to the shed, Pap was ... Pap was standin' on a chair with that rope tied around his neck.

"He said ... he said, 'Don't come near me boy! I mean it, don't come near me!' Then he said, 'Tell your Momma ... tell her I'm sorry son. Sorry for everything. I love you Noah. Always remember that.'"

Sobs erupted from Noah then. Looking at his mother in despair, he whispered, "I tried to stop him Momma! I tried! I thought I wanted him dead, I was even gonna do it myself ... but then ... then ... when I saw ... what he was gonna do ... I didn't want him to do it! I swear!

"He wouldn't let me get near him. He kept kickin' at me every time I tried. Then he kicked me so hard I fell ... and then before I could get up he kicked the chair out from under him ... and ... I heard somethin' snap, and then ... he just stopped movin'. I was so scared I didn't know what to do, so I just ran, I just kept runnin' and runnin'.

"Oh Momma! I didn't mean for this to happen! You believe that don't you?" Noah wailed.

Sarah wrapped her arms around her son. Rocking him back and forth, she said, "I believe you Noah. I believe you."

A moment later Tommy came into the living room. In a raspy voice still sore from the throttling he'd received the previous night, he asked, "What's wrong? What's the matter Noah?"

Patting the sofa next to her, Sarah said, "C'mere son," then, "Tommy ... Noble's dead. He hanged himself last night."

For several seconds, Tommy stared wide-eyed at Sarah, than broke down in tears.

Lifting his chin gently, she said, "It's gonna be all right."

Then she hugged both boys tightly to her.

After they had quieted, she said, "I'm gonna go out and cut your Pap down ..."

"No! I'll do it!"

"No. I'm gonna do it. I want you to get cleaned up, and stay in here with Tommy. I won't be long."

Sarah took a deep breath to steady her nerves before she entered the shed. Averting her eyes from the body, she walked purposefully to Noble's bench and picked up the hacksaw.

Noble had tied the rope around a leg of the work bench which was bolted solidly to the wall, then looped it several times over the exposed beam.

All Sarah had to do to get him down was saw through the knotted hemp attached to the bench. Unfortunately, her hands trembled so violently she could hardly hold onto the saw.

It took an agonizingly long time for her to complete the task, but eventually she did. When Noble's body hit the floor with a sickening thud, Sarah turned and ran to him. Then she fell to her knees beside him and pulled his head into her lap.

As she cradled him tightly she cried out, "Oh Noble! Why did it have to come to this?"

Tommy followed Noah to the bathroom and as he watched him splash cold water over his face, he said, "Noah ... you think if you wish for somethin' hard enough ... it can come true?"

At first Noah just shrugged his shoulders noncommittally and continued splashing cold water onto his face.

"I mean, if you wish for somethin' bad to happen to somebody ... and then somethin' bad happens to 'em ..."

Noah stopped then and turned toward the younger boy.

"Li'l Bit, if wishes were horses beggars would ride. If wishin' made it so, Pap would've been gone a long time ago, cuz you weren't the only one wishin' he'd go away."

As Sarah walked back to the house, a welcome numbness settled over her.

She realized she wouldn't be able to move Noble alone and since Noah and Tommy had been through enough torment in the last twenty-four hours to last them a lifetime, she made the decision to go into town for help.

There was only one person in the entire town of Dawson Sarah felt she could turn to — Ida Anderson, the owner of Ida's Cafe.

Ida regularly bought chickens from Sarah and always had, depending on the weather, a hot cup of coffee or a cold glass of tea waiting for her, along with warm and welcome conversation. Sarah genuinely treasured the older woman's friendship.

Ida and her husband Birdie, now deceased, were one of only two African-American families living in Dawson. Reverend and Mrs. Hickey and their brood, five children in all, were the other, and as equally loved and respected as the Andersons.

Mrs. Norma Hickey taught at the school, while her husband, Reverend Darby Hickey, served as the town's pastor.

So after cleaning herself up, Sarah warned the boys to stay inside until she returned, and then she left for Ida's.

After pulling into the alley behind Ida's Cafe, Sarah sat pensively behind the wheel until she finally summoned the courage to go inside. When she walked through the back door to the kitchen, Sam Clemens, Ida's dishwasher, was the first to notice her. By the look on his face, Sarah knew she must have looked pretty bad. He quickly dropped the pan he was washing back into the sink and hurried over to her.

Drying his soapy hands on his apron, he said, "Miz Sarah, what's wrong? What's happened?"

"Mr. Clemens I gotta talk to Miz Ida, is she here?"

"Sure, sure, I'll go get her," he said, wrapping a scrawny arm comfortingly around her as he led her to a chair.

"Here Miz Sarah, you just sit right here. I'll be back shortly."

By then Walter Bizby, Ida's cook, heard the commotion and came to see what was going on. Taking in Sarah's disheveled appearance, he asked with concern, "Ya'll right Miz Sarah?"

Sarah hesitated for a moment, though she wished it otherwise, the whole town of Dawson was bound to find out about Noble's suicide.

"No Mr. Bizby, I'm not. My husband, Noble, hanged himself."

Sucking his breath in loudly, Walter said, "God Almighty! Oh Miz Sarah, I surely am sorry!"

About that time Ida and Sam came barreling through the kitchen. One look at Sarah, and Ida, never one to mince words, blurted out, "What in the sam hell happened to you honey?"

Before Sarah could tell her, Walter rushed in, "Miz Ida, Noble McAllister's done gone and hanged himself!"

At sixty-two, there wasn't much that could rattle Ida Anderson's composure, and this was no exception.

"Why that no account good for nothin' sod! Figures that dang fool would go off and do somethin' stupid like this!" She hissed at the same time she enveloped the younger woman in her ample arms.

Without so much as taking a breath, Ida continued, "What can we do? How can we help?"

"Well, I can't move Noble by myself. He's ... he's still in the shed ... where it happened ... so I guess ..." Sarah stammered.

"Walter, you go on back to work. Kitty can handle what's left of the morning crowd. Sam you come with me.

Walter, if anybody asks where we're at, you just tell 'em we're out runnin' errands, and don't mention anything about this to anybody. Got it?"

"You can count on me Miz Ida," Walter said with a nod.

Grabbing the car keys from the pegboard on the wall, Ida headed out the back door with Sam and Sarah in tow.

In prosperity our friends know us;
In adversity we know our friends.

— Churton Collins

Chapter Nine

Upon hearing the pick-up roll into the yard, Noah and Tommy came out onto the porch. Both watched silently as Ida and Sam, who pulled up behind Sarah in Ida's big Buick, got out and approached Sarah.

For a few moments they discussed something the boys could not hear. Then Sarah got out and all three walked toward them.

When Ida and Sam were close enough to see Noah's face and the ugly marks on Tommy's neck, Ida at least had the good sense to keep her thoughts to herself. Sam however, sucked his breath in loudly and said, "Jimany Christmas! What in the heck went on here last night?"

"Sam!" Ida admonished.

Sarah began to explain, but Ida cut her off.

"Honey, first things first. Go get a sheet so Sam and I can get Noble to the truck. There'll be plenty of time later for details."

Reluctantly, Sarah allowed Ida to convince her to stay inside with the boys while she and Sam took care of the business of moving Noble.

"C'mon Sam, let's get this done and over with," Ida said as she stepped through the doorway of the workshed.

One look at Noble's bloated, discolored face, caused Sam to double over and begin gagging uncontrollably.

"Oh my goodness!" he spewed, still heaving.

"Sam Clemens get a hold of yourself!" Ida snapped, though she too felt queasiness nearly overtake her.

It wasn't just the sight of Noble, it was also the smell of death that permeated the confining, hot, humid shed. It was almost more than either could bear.

Eventually, the two were able to move past the shock and revulsion. And Ida at least, was able to focus on the task ahead of them.

Seeing the rope still wrapped around Noble's neck, Ida said, "Sam, get over here and help me get this rope off his neck."

"Uh, uh. I ... I can't. You do it Miz Ida." Sam said weakly, as he leaned heavily on the workbench, fearing he was going to pass out from the horrendous stench alone.

Ida shot her dishwasher a scathing look of contempt. Then she took a deep breath, mumbled something about him being useless, and steeled herself to do the job alone.

Once done, Ida said caustically, "Do you think you can at least throw me the sheet? ... Now don't strain yourself."

"I'm sorry Miz Ida, truly. It's just, just that I ain't never seen nothin' like this before." Sam whined guiltily.

"I know Sam, me either. It's all right."

Ida spread the sheet out next to Noble. "Sam I can't lift him alone, you're gonna have to help me here."

"Okay. okay. Just give me a minute," Sam said as he nervously wiped the sweat from his brow, took a steadying breath then walked purposefully to the foot of Noble's body.

"On the count of three, lift him onto the sheet, then grab the corners and we'll carry him like that to the truck."

"Yep. I'm ready when you are Miz Ida," Sam said, turning his face away from the body and trying not to take too deep a breath as he grabbed hold of Noble's booted heels.

It took all of their combined strength to carry Noble's corpse awkwardly to the truck. They nearly dropped him twice and Ida sincerely hoped Sarah and her children were not watching from the windows.

Just as the thought ran through Ida's mind, Noah peered through the curtain again, visibly wincing when they almost dropped his father for the second time. Another wave of guilt washed over him. He should be the one performing this, perhaps final task for his father, not strangers.

"Momma, please let me go out there and help them with Pap," Noah asked again.

"Noah, it's better this way. It won't be much longer now," Sarah assured him gently.

Maneuvering Noble into the back of the truck was not easy. As Ida tried to lift his head and shoulders high enough to clear the tailgate, Sam surged forward before she was ready, which caused Noble's head to slam into the back of the pick-up. Thankfully, no one was watching from the windows then.

Both were mindful that what they held was once a living, breathing human being. Neither was intentionally being disrespectful.

However, it was not a walk in the park for an elderly woman and a rail-thin, five-foot-five man to transport a six-foot-two, two-hundred-ten-pound body with nothing more than a tattered sheet. And it took them nearly half an hour to accomplish the task.

Afterward, they took several moments to collect themselves. Leaning against the truck with sweat dripping from every pore, Sam said breathlessly, "So what are we gonna do now Miz Ida?"

"Well, I'll let Sarah know we're done and get another sheet to throw over the top of Noble. Then I guess we'll take him to Farley's Funeral Home."

"Miz Ida, what do you think folks are gonna say when they see those boys?"

Ida sighed heavily.

"I honestly don't know. I suspect some won't care one way or another. Certainly some are gonna jump to the conclusion that there's more here than meets the eye. But here's what I am sure of Sam — the McAllisters need our help, and I'm determined to give it to them!" Ida finished with conviction.

"I'm with you on that Miz Ida," Sam said. Then he retrieved a rather crumpled pack of cigarettes out of his shirt pocket, tapped it against his hand and pulled one out. Just before lighting the filterless stick he looked at Ida for a long, silent moment.

"What do you think really happened Miz Ida? You think Miz Sarah and her boys did him in?"

"I'm gonna save judgement until I here the whole story Sam. I recommend you do the same. Things aren't always what they seem.

"Anyway, why don't you stay out here and finish your smoke, I'll go get another sheet, and see what Sarah wants to do now."

After tapping lightly on the door, Ida entered the house. Noah was still standing at the window which caused Ida's face to flush guiltily, realizing Noah must've witnessed their unintentional rough handling of his father after all.

"Sarah, could you get me another sheet to throw over top ... over top of ... Noble?"

As Sarah brought her the sheet, Ida searched the younger woman's face for a moment, then said, "I suppose we'll be takin' Noble to Farley's?"

"I, I guess so."

Suddenly Sarah's face drained of color, and with great difficulty she said haltingly, "Miz Ida? I don't have any ... money to give Mr. Farley for a funeral."

"Now don't you go concernin' yourself with that nonsense. We'll figure it out later," Ida rushed in. Knowing how difficult times were for the McAllisters made her heart ache for them.

"Sarah, why don't I ride with you over to Farley's? That way I can send Sam back to the cafe and the boys can stay here 'til we take care of this business."

"Okay,"

"No!" Noah said forcefully from across the room, causing both women to jerk their heads toward him at the same time.

"Momma, I'll go with you to Farley's."

Sarah considered Noah's request for several moments, finally she said, "Noah, honey, listen to me. I know you think you owe this to your Pap, but I need you here. Who else is gonna stay to look after Tommy?"

Noah could not explain to his mother, especially in front of Ida, the overwhelming sense of obligation he felt. Even though he knew she was right, it didn't stop guilt from gnawing at his conscience.

Sarah could see the emotional turmoil in Noah's eyes. And she wished more than anything that she could protect him from this pain.

Finally Noah shook his head, conceding to his mother's wishes.

Sam took one last, long drag on his cigarette as Ida and Sarah approached the truck. Though he would have been hard-pressed to explain it, he couldn't look Sarah in the eyes. In an attempt to cover up his uncomfortableness, he busied himself with the task of stomping out his cigarette butt on the ground. When Ida told him to go back to the cafe and not say a word to anyone, he was more than happy to oblige.

He opened the door to the Buick and started to get in, then stopped mid way, without turning back to look at the two women, he said, "Miz Sarah ... I really am sorry about this. If there's anything I can do ..."

"Thank you Sam, I appreciate that," Sarah replied, choking back tears.

Without another word he got in the car and drove off.

Moments later, Sarah and Ida left for Farley's.

After several moments of awkward silence, Ida said, "Well honey, I guess now is as good a time as any for details."

Taking a deep breath, Sarah began. By the time she was finished, she had told Ida everything that had transpired from the time Noble came home drunk, until the moment she pulled up behind the cafe. There was only one small detail Sarah changed – the part where Noble had shouted at Tommy that his family had been right to throw him away. She substituted with, "he had been nothing but trouble since they took him in".

Ida digested her story quietly, slowly, then offered, "Sarah, I'm gonna tell you the truth as I see it, because I wouldn't be doin' you any favors otherwise.

"When this gets out and folks get a look at the marks on your boys, people are gonna talk. You gotta know that."

"I know."

"Good. I just want you to be prepared."

After another stretch of uneasy silence, Ida continued, "Honey, there's somethin' else. Somethin' I think you already know ... but I'm gonna say it just the same."

Sarah braced herself.

Picking her words carefully, Ida started with, "Sarah, Walter and Sam, I'm sad to say, were involved in that dirty business with those drifters ten years ago, just like Noble."

Knowing her words would be difficult for the younger woman to hear, Ida paused for a moment to give Sarah a chance to absorb the direction of the conversation.

"At first they stuck with the story that had been concocted at Carter's farm about never findin' those two people. But they were actin' so strange after it all happened, I knew there was more to it, and it didn't take me long to drag it out of them. When I did, they told me everything from start to finish. They told me about Tipton shootin' the girl, and then how nearly everybody tore into that Leonard. They even told me how Noble had jumped in the middle of it and tried to stop it.

"Well, when those investigators came around askin' questions, I kept my mouth shut for Sam and Walter's sake ... and for my own reasons too," Ida added cryptically.

She hesitated as though she were trying to make up her mind about something. Eventually she continued with, "Anyway, everybody knows there was bad blood between Ernest and Noble after that. Some actually know why, and some only think they do. It's also no secret that Ernest has had it in for your Noah since he beat the sense out of his boy Billy."

Ida chuckled softly at the memory, "I can tell you, there were more than a few overjoyed parents when they heard about the well-deserved spankin' Noah gave that bully.

"My point is — it shouldn't come as any surprise that Tipton will probably try and make a mountain out of this mole hill. Are you ready for that Sarah?"

Releasing a long, disheartened sigh, Sarah replied, "Miz Ida, I'm not ready for any of this, but since the choice is not mine to make, I'm just gonna do my best to take it as it comes and hang on to the truth. And the truth is, Noble hanged himself."

"I know that, but I want you to weigh what I'm about to say very carefully, because I have known Ernest Tipton his entire life, and I can tell you for a fact that he can be a sneaky, vindictive S.O.B. I've seen it first-hand.

"Luckily for you, he's also a coward, and when push comes to shove, given the right incentive, Ernest'll back down. I believe that incentive is to remind him of the past. Let him know straight away if he causes you or your family one ounce of trouble over this, you won't hesitate to tell what you know to anybody who'll listen … let him know you'll go all the way to Atlanta if need be," Ida finished firmly.

Weary beyond measure, Sarah whispered, "What about everybody else involved? What would happen to them?"

"Don't worry about them. Ernest won't let it go that far. After all, remember, he is the one who shot and killed that girl. And as the sheriff, he should've stopped those men before they beat that Leonard to death, but he didn't. If all of that isn't bad enough, according to Walter and Sam, burying the bodies and the evidence and keepin' quiet about it all was Ernest's idea. Now who do you think the law's gonna come down hardest on? It would be Ernest of course, and he would know that.

"That's why I believe if you put on a brave face and stand your ground, he'll cry 'uncle' long before you do. I guarantee it!"

Because of Tommy, Sarah knew she could never risk confronting or threatening Ernest as Ida suggested, though she could never reveal that to her.

"Maybe you're wrong. Maybe Ernest'll just leave us alone," Sarah ventured weakly.

"Hmmm, not likely, but I guess anything's possible."

More awkward silence followed. Then just before they turned onto the final stretch of road that would take them into town and then to Farley's, Ida said, "Sarah, pull over here and let's stop for a minute."

After shutting off the engine Sarah quietly waited for Ida to speak.

Finally, Ida ventured, "This is not gonna be easy to hear, so steady yourself. I know why you might be afraid to threaten Ernest with the past — because of Tommy. Because of who he really is."

Sarah felt the blood completely drain from her face. An instant headache the size of Texas began to assault her temples. It was so severe that it temporarily blurred her vision.

"WWWhat?" was the only word she could vocalize. Suddenly, Sarah felt every bit like a deer caught in the headlights of an oncoming car, knowing it was about to be crushed beneath the vehicle, yet completely powerless to move out of its way.

Ida took a deep breath. Slowly, deliberately, she repeated, "I said ... I know who Tommy really is."

Sarah opened her mouth to speak, but nothing came out.

Ida patted her hand reassuringly, "First, let me ease your mind and tell you, I believe I'm the only one in Dawson who knows, and as God is my witness, I will never tell another living soul. So relax honey and just listen to what I have to say."

Ida allowed the distraught woman a moment to take in this revelation, then continued, "For the few weeks those drifters were workin' for Harvey, that girl, Missy was her name, would come to the cafe to get food for the two of them.

"I bet that poor little thing couldn't have been more then sixteen, and I'm pretty sure that cradle robbin' lowlife she called Leonard, had already seen the best side of forty. But I didn't meet him 'til later.

"Anyway, one day I asked her whereabouts she lived, she got so scared I thought for a second she was just gonna turn around and run out the door, but she didn't. She stammered and stuttered for a bit, but finally she told me they were stayin' just outside of town.

"Well of course being the busybody I am, I wanted to know where exactly. It took some doin' but eventually I got her to describe the area well enough that I realized it could only be where old man Miller use to live.

"Now, I'm really curious because I know that old shack's been abandoned since Morgan Miller died fifteen years before. But I didn't say anything to Missy.

"After she left, I told myself I was gonna have to go have a talk with Harvey to see what he knew about those two, but as it turned out I never got the chance. Anyhow, the next evening just before I closed up, she came in actin' mighty nervous.

"She got an order to go like usual, then she lays a quarter on the counter and smiles. Then she leans in close and she says, 'Leonard don't know I got that.' Then she looks at me real serious and says, 'Ma'am, you think I got enough there to buy a little cup of milk and maybe an extra piece of bread? My baby ...' Then she gets this horrified look on her face and shuts up.

"I gave her the milk and bread and told her to hang on to her money. Of course now I'm more curious than ever and even more determined to find out what was going on out there.

"So after I closed up, I wrapped up some leftovers and headed out to old man Miller's. It took me awhile to find the place because I hadn't been out that way in ages.

"Let me tell you Sarah, those people were livin' in such squalid conditions not fit for animals, let alone people, and definitely not suitable for a baby.

"Anyway, I picked my way through the junk and the garbage and when I got to the porch, I heard somethin' mewlin'. At first I thought it was a cat. But the closer I got the more I was convinced it couldn't be a cat.

"When I got close enough to poke my head through a busted window, I saw that baby Missy mentioned. They had him in an old wooden crate, he was just lyin' there all curled up like a little pill bug, and that's where the noise was comin' from.

"I guess they had been leavin' that little boy alone like that all day long while they were at Harvey's station.

"Can you imagine that? I can't recall a time past or present when I've been that mad. To see that poor little mite like that, well, there just aren't words, that's all.

"Anyhow, I called out to Missy, then waited. Nothin'. So I called out again, and pretty soon after, Missy and that sorry excuse for a man came walkin' around the side of the shack tuckin' their clothes in.

"Just about that time that little boy starts cryin' pretty loud. That slimy rat shoves Missy hard and he says, 'Go shut that kid up 'fore I shut him up permanent!'

"Then he gives me this hateful look and says, 'What're you doin' here?'

"Sarah, have you ever seen pure evil? I think I did that day. I believe I saw it when I looked into that Leonard's beady black eyes. Truly, that man made my skin crawl. I'm ashamed to say it, but I was scared. Scared for my very life.

"When he took a step toward me I came so close to droppin' the food I held and then just runnin'. I didn't, though I still don't know how I managed to keep my composer. I told him I had leftovers from the diner and thought he and his wife wouldn't mind takin' them off my hands.

"While he's standing there starin' me down I could actually see his nostrils flare, it made my blood run cold, truly.

"Anyway, he said, 'How'd you know we were here?' I said 'Missy told me'. By the look that came over his face I knew she was gonna pay for that later, and I felt awful. So I held out the plate of food and said, 'You don't have to worry, I'm not gonna tell anyone you're out here.

"Nobody would care anyway. I just didn't want this food to go to waste ... so I thought ...' Before I could finish, he snatched the plate from me and said, 'You best get on outta here and don't come back! Then he added, 'If you know what's good for you, you won't say nothin' to nobody about us bein' out here!'

"He didn't have to tell me twice. I was out of there before he turned around to go back inside that shack. I'll tell you Sarah, I was shakin' like a leaf as I drove home, thankin' the good Lord the whole way.

"I didn't calm down until I woke up the next morning. By then I had made up my mind I was gonna get Walter and Sam to go out there with me after we closed up the diner and get that baby. Maybe Missy too if I could talk her in to leavin' him. All I said to Walter and Sam was that I had somethin' I needed their help with after we closed up.

"Of course that was the same day the Petersons were murdered. I still can't figure how Harvey came to hire someone like that Leonard, even for a short time. I'll tell you Sarah, I have never been able to forgive myself for not rattin' those people out that night. I keep thinkin' maybe if I had, poor old Harv and Edna would still be alive.

"Well, shoulda, coulda, woulda. All I know is, I'll live with the guilt until my dyin' day.

"Anyhow, when Sam and Walter finally came clean and told me what happened with that Leonard and Missy, they never mentioned anything about a baby.

"I felt so mixed up about it all I didn't want to say anything until I knew for sure what had happened to that little boy. So I went back out to the Miller shack thinkin' they had left him there to starve to death. When I didn't find him, I was beside myself. And honestly, by then I was too afraid and ashamed to tell anyone. I mean, in my confused state of mind, I actually thought that if people found out I had known about that baby before the Petersons were killed, I don't know. Maybe they'd think I was somehow responsible, or involved, or ... well, all that sounds crazy to me now, but at the time I just wasn't thinkin' straight.

"Then of course, it wasn't long after, that you told me about the little boy you and Noble had taken in when your cousins died in that fire. Of course, as soon as I saw him I knew who he really was.

"Although, he sure looked a lot different and a lot healthier than the first time I saw him, I still recognized him. Sarah, you don't know how close I came to telling you about my run-in with his folks. But I decided that was something better left for me to know and no one else to find out. And I was happy to leave it that way until now.

"And the only reason I bring it up now is so that you'll understand I am the only person alive that could possibly know the truth, and I will take it to my grave. So don't be afraid to stand up to Ernest when and if the time comes, because you really don't have anything to lose."

Ida's confession of being afraid to reveal the truth for fear of being implicated in the tragedies, was hauntingly familiar to Sarah as she mentally began to relive that day so long ago.

"Noah found him after he got off the bus that day. Those people had just left him in that crate on the side of the road. Left him there like he was nothin' more than garbage to be disposed of.

"Noah was so excited when he came burstin' through the door screamin' for me to come see what he had found.

"We couldn't believe it at first. Who leaves a baby on the side of the road like that? But when Noah took his Pap back to where he had found him, we knew he was tellin' the truth.

"I stayed behind and cleaned Tommy up. He was so filthy. He had bruises, big ones, all over his body. I swore to myself I wasn't gonna let that poor baby go back to whoever had done that to him. They didn't deserve him, and didn't want him anyway, I told myself.

"Noble remembered those people from Harvey's station, he thought Tommy resembled the man he called Leonard. So he went to the station to talk to Harvey to see what he could find out. That's when he found the Petersons. And you know what happened after that.

"Like you Miz Ida, after everything that happened we were too scared to speak up and tell the truth. So I came up with that story about my cousins. At first Noble didn't want to go along with it. He wanted to get rid of Tommy. He wanted to ... well, it doesn't matter now."

After a momentary silence, Sarah hung her head, put her hands to her face and cried.

Ida leaned over and enveloped her gently in her arms.

"Honey, you go ahead and cry all you want, just get it all out."

For several moments Ida continued with reassuring words of comfort until Sarah was able to collect herself.

"Sarah, Lord knows you and your family have been through enough, and, unfortunately, we both know it's not over yet. But I want you to know I'll do whatever I can to help you and your boys. And if Ernest Tipton does try to cause you any grief over this, we'll deal with him together. You won't have to face him alone."

"Thank you Miz Ida," Sarah replied with heartfelt sincerity.

People grow through experience
if they meet life honestly and courageously.
This is how character is built.

— Eleanor Roosevelt

Chapter Ten

In a small town like Dawson, business was always slow for an undertaker, so out of shear boredom, Paul, Carl Farley's son, had devised a list of Farley's potential customers, their approximate date of arrival, and probable cause of death.

Most of those on the list were elderly or infirm, and though many would have considered his private game a perverse one, he saw it as a harmless way to wile away the endless boring hours.

As he sat at the front desk meticulously going over his list, Ida and Sarah came in. Caught off-guard by the unexpected visit, Paul's face turned a guilty shade of red, and he suddenly felt as though he had just been caught with his pants down around his knees.

Recovering quickly, he asked with professional politeness, "Miz Anderson, Miz McAllister, what can I do for you ladies today?"

"Where's your daddy Paul?"

"He's in the back Miz Anderson. If you ladies wanna have a seat over there I'll get him for you," Paul said, pointing toward several ornate, yet well-worn chairs in the corner of the room. He tried not to show his disappointment at having to wait to hear what had brought the unlikely pair to the funeral home.

A short time later, Carl came out to greet them. At five feet eight inches, fifty-five-year-old Carl Farley was nearly as wide as he was tall, yet surprisingly agile for a man of his size. Due to good genes, he still retained a full head of thick hair, and the salt and pepper color gave him a serious, distinguished look, which belied his often comedic nature.

Carl had been a regular customer at the cafe for nearly forty years and Ida liked him. His healthy sense of humor always amused her, especially given his line of work.

Smiling with genuine warmth, Carl said, "Ida, Mrs. McAllister, what brings you two ladies out on this fine day?"

"Do you have someplace private we can talk Carl?" Ida asked.

"Sure, we can go to my office," he said, gesturing for the two to follow him.

After Sarah and Ida were seated, Carl waited patiently for one of them to speak.

"Carl, Noble McAllister hanged himself last night. We have him outside in the pick-up."

"Oh Mrs. McAllister, I truly am sorry," Carl said with genuine sympathy, hoping the shock he felt didn't register on his face.

"Mrs. McAllister ... Dr. Hadley and ... the sheriff ... have been notified, haven't they?"

"No. Why?" Ida blurted out.

"Well Ida, there's certain procedures you have to follow in a death such as this. Suicide's against the law you know."

"Carl Farley, what are you talkin' about?" Ida asked with growing irritation.

"Now Ida, don't kill the messenger for bringing the message. In the state of Georgia, suicide's considered a crime. That means the law has to be notified, and Ben Hadley's gonna have to examine the bod ... Mr. McAllister, to determine the cause and time of death. So he can fill out a death certificate before I can prepare Mr. McAllister for burial," Carl said uncomfortably.

Ida glanced sideways at Sarah to see how she was holding up. Judging by the look on her face, she wasn't doing very well.

Placing a consoling hand over one of hers, Ida said, "Carl, this poor woman's been through enough for one day. Now, go ahead and call Ben over here so he can do whatever needs to be done. Of course he's gonna tell you, just like me — Noble McAllister hanged himself! End of story.

"About that other nonsense, well, that just doesn't make any sense. How does the law punish a person for killin' himself?

"I'd say the good Lord will do that just fine without any interference from us! So why don't we just leave the sheriff out of this?"

"Ida, I can't do it. It's against the law. In a situation like this, foul play has to be ruled out, that's why Doc Hadley and Sheriff Tipton have to be notified.

"I'm sorry. Mrs. McAllister, I truly am. I don't want to cause you any more upset, but I hope you can understand my position."

"Carl, could you give us a minute?"

"Certainly," Carl said, then excused himself from the room.

Looking at Sarah critically, Ida said, "Honey, we knew this was likely to happen. So we're gonna have to just buck up and handle it. One step at a time."

Within a few minutes, Dr. Ben Hadley and Sheriff Ernest Tipton arrived at the funeral home. After Carl gave them a brief summary of his conversation with the two women, they went out to the pick-up.

A suspended hush filled the air as Carl lifted the sheet from Noble. The smell of death was almost unbearable, and all three men covered their mouths to lessen the stench as they stared down at the body.

Tipton was the first to break the silence. Clicking his tongue disapprovingly he said, "Well, would you look at that," pointing to the wound on Noble's arm.

"Suicide huh?" He continued with a sneer.

"All right, that's enough Tipton." Ben said irritably. He didn't like Ernest Tipton, nor did he have any respect whatsoever for the town's sheriff.

He could never understand why the people of Dawson kept re-electing the incompetent knucklehead. As far as Ben was concerned, the only thing Tipton was good for was stirring up trouble.

Just last month Ben had had to intercede on his nurse, Josephine's, behalf with her neighbor Ike Mooney. When Tipton found Jo's friendly hound Rascal running loose in the neighborhood, he had gone straight to Ike, a man known around town for his hot headedness. He informed him that Rascal had gotten out and Ike should look out for his chickens. And oh by the way, should the good for nothing hound wander onto his property, he would be well within his rights to shoot the mangy mutt — in protection of his livestock of course.

Then Tipton returned Rascal to his owner with a stern warning that her neighbors were not going to put up with her dog roaming free in the neighborhood And in fact, one had even threatened to shoot him.

Jo did not have to ask who he was referring to. When the tension between Ike and Jo escalated into shouting matches over the fence line that separated their properties, Ben offered to intervene. That's when he got to the bottom of the story and found out Tipton had put the idea of shooting Rascal into Ike's head.

"Carl, take him inside.

"Where is Mrs. McAllister? I want to check on her, see if she needs anything, then I'll examine Mr. McAllister."

"Hold on there Doc, you need to take care of this business first. I'm sure the missus is just fine, can't imagine she'd be mournin' the loss of this lowlife drunkard anyway," Tipton finished sarcastically.

Ben slammed his hand down hard on the pick-up.

"Listen you pea brain little rat! I don't take orders from you. So shut up and stay out of my way Tipton!

"And by the way, I wonder how many people would mourn your sorry butt if that was you lying there instead of Noble McAllister!" Ben lashed out angrily as he pushed past the speechless officer.

Tipton stared after the doctor red-faced, though he wisely kept his mouth shut as he had been advised.

Then he turned toward Carl and barked, "What are you lookin' at? Go on and do like the Doc said!"

Ben found Sarah and Ida where Carl had left them in his office.

He pulled up a chair beside Sarah, patted her hand comfortingly and said, "Mrs. McAllister, I'm very sorry for your loss."

Reaching into his black medical bag, he pulled out a small bottle of pills and continued, "These are sedatives to help you get some rest. I want you to go home and take two of these with a glass of water. I'm going to give you enough to last a few days so take them as you need them, but don't take more than four in a twenty-four hour period.

"If you need anything else just let me know."

Turning to Ida he asked, "Where are the boys?"

"At the farm."

"Ben, might I have a word with you outside?"

Giving Sarah's shoulder a gentle squeeze, Ida said, "Honey, I'll be right back."

Ida liked Ben, even more than Carl. Not only was he a fine doctor, but he had a good heart, and Ida believed he was about as fair minded as a man could be. That's why she felt comfortable asking for his help.

"Ben, the McAllisters are in a real bad spot here. Now, it's a fact that Noble hanged himself, but when people get a look at those boys they're gonna wonder if he didn't have a little help preparing for his journey to meet our maker. And that Ernest Tipton's gonna have a field day with this."

Ida then gave Ben a brief recounting of what had transpired the previous night at the McAllister farm, just as Sarah had told it to her.

"I'm sure you know there's been bad blood between that family and Ernest for a very long time, and this is just the sort of thing that slimy weasel lives for."

Ben shook his head sympathetically and said, "Tell Mrs. McAllister not to worry, I'll do whatever I can to help. In the mean time, why don't you take her home. As soon as I finish up here, I'll come out to the farm and check on them."

"Thanks Ben.

"You're a good ol' egg you know that?"

Ben smiled, gave Ida an affectionate pat on the back, then left her to find Carl and Ernest.

It didn't take Ben long to locate the men, and as he stepped through the doorway, he overheard Tipton remark, "I'm just surprised nobody did this skunk in sooner!"

Carl scowled disapprovingly, yet kept quiet. He didn't like the sheriff any better than Hadley did, but unlike the doctor, he didn't have the courage to rebuke him, for he knew only too well from their school days what a tormenting bully Tipton could be.

That mean streak had only gotten worse with age and position, and crossing the sheriff of Dawson could mean weeks, if not months of unrelenting harassment. Carl knew more than a few people in town that could testify to that. Better to hold his tongue and keep the peace he decided.

Relieved to see Ben and turn Noble's body over to him, Carl said, "All right Dr. Hadley we'll leave you to it then," and headed for the door.

When Ernest didn't follow behind Farley, Ben said, "That means you too Tipton."

"Oh no Ben, you see I believe we might have a real crime on our hands. And this body is evidence, and that means I stay."

Ben had to fight an almost uncontrollable urge to punch Tipton squarely in the face. Then just for pure pleasure, physically throw him out of the room. Fortunately for Ernest, better judgement prevailed and though it rankled him greatly, Ben had to acknowledge the sheriff's right to be present at the autopsy.

"All right you can stay, as long as you stand over there and keep your mouth shut. I'm warning you Ernest, if you even so much as sneeze out loud, you're out of here!" Ben said as he pointed to the farthest corner in the room.

To Carl, Ben said, "Can you see if you can catch up with Ida before she leaves, I need to have a quick word with her."

Carl, grateful to have any reason to excuse himself from the tension-filled atmosphere, replied, "Right away Ben."

Ida had just started the truck when she caught sight of Carl waving his arms frantically from the doorway.

Unable to hear him over the din of the engine, Ida turned it off and waited for Carl to reach them.

"Ida, Ben would like to have a word with you before you take off."

"What for?"

"I don't know he didn't say."

Ida gave Sarah a half smile and said, "Just sit tight, I'll be back in a minute."

Upon entering the room, Ida immediately noticed Tipton skulking in the corner. As his beady eyes darted from Ben to her and back again, she could almost see the wheels spinning in his tiny little brain. It left no doubt in her mind that he was already conspiring against Sarah and her sons.

"Ben, you wanted to see me?"

Turning to Ida and away from Tipton, Ben gave her a cautionary look, picked up his medical bag and as he walked toward her said, "I forgot to give you the sedatives for Mrs. McAllister."

Then with a gentle hand he took hold of her elbow and guided her out of the room, closing the door behind them.

In a low voice, Ben said, "You were right, Tipton is definitely going to cause trouble for that family. If those boys look as bad as you say they do, I'm afraid they might have something to worry about."

"I knew it!"

"So I would like to see them before Tipton does. Since he'll probably head straight for the McAllisters after we're through here, see if Mrs. McAllister will let you bring her children back with you. Take them to my house, Hannah's home so she'll let you in. Just tell her there was an accident and I'll explain the rest when I get home.

"If you tell Mrs. McAllister that you're taking the boys to your house, that's what she'll tell Tipton, and by sending him on a goose chase, that should buy the time I need to examine their injuries.

"I'll keep Tipton with me as long as I can. In fact, I'll go with him to the farm, that ought to slow down any mischief he intends, at least temporarily. By the time he actually locates the boys, I'm sure we'll have come up with a way to stop, or at least temper any trouble he might cause.

"I'll do it Ben."

The look of concern on Sarah's face as Ida approached the truck prompted her to say, "Honey wipe that scared look off your face, it was nothin'.

"Ben just wanted to make sure I make you take those pills he gave you so you can get some rest. And that's exactly what I'm gonna do. And I'm gonna take your boys back to my house, get them somthin' to eat and take care of them for the rest of the day so you can get some rest."

"I appreciate that Miz Ida, but I don't want to be away from my boys right now. They need me. We need each other."

"Now Sarah, I won't hear another word about it! You need some rest. They need to eat. I'll take good care of your babies, don't you worry about that. Besides, gettin' away from there for awhile just might be the best thing for them."

Sarah mulled it over for a few moments, "I know you're right, but they won't go."

"Well, we'll just see about that!"

As Ben made some final notes, Tipton, who had been surprisingly silent, asked, "So what do you think Ben?"

Not bothering to stop writing or look up, the doctor replied, "Cause of death, broken neck. Self-inflicted. End of story."

"Well what about that gash on his arm? That self-inflicted too?" Tipton asked sarcastically.

"Ernest, I'm sorry to disappoint you, but the only crime that's been committed here, is that this man felt so hopeless he took his own life. It was clearly suicide. And the wound on his arm had nothing to do with his death, so it doesn't matter how it happened.

"After a thorough examination there is no evidence whatsoever to indicate Noble McAllister died by anything other than his own hand. So leave it alone and do something decent for a change, and let this family mourn their dead and move on, all right?"

Before Ernest could respond, Carl and Jess Spencer burst into the room. Jesses' shirt was soaked with blood and his face was drained of all color.

Gasping for air, he said, "Doc, we need your help! My hired hand Erin got his arm caught in the baler. We got it free but it's chewed up pretty bad and we can't stop the bleeding. We gotta hurry Doc, I've already wasted enough time just tryin' to find you!"

112

All of a sudden Jess sucked his breath in loudly, as he realized in that instant who was lying on the table.

"Lord Almighty! What happened to Noble?" he asked in shock.

Ben didn't say anything as he grabbed his medical bag and started for the door. Then he stopped, turned toward Ernest and said, "C'mon Tipton we'll take your squad car."

"Sorry Ben, I got other business to attend to. 'Sides, nothin' I can do for Erin."

Swearing angrily under his breath, Ben said to Carl, "Go ahead and prepare Mr. McAllister for burial." Then as he began to follow Jess out of the room he threw over his shoulder, "Stick around Ernest. We're not through with this conversation."

As Carl held the door open for Jess and Ben, he watched as a slow, menacing smile spread across Ernest's face. To Ben's departing back he sneered just loud enough for Carl to hear, "Whatever you say Doc."

Carl cleared his throat to get Tipton's attention, and to indicate he was still holding the door open for him to leave as well.

Scowling angrily at the undertaker, Ernest said, "Hold your horses there fat man, I'm goin'."

When he was at the door and next to Carl, Tipton made a jerking movement toward him as though he were going to hit him. When Carl jumped back in surprise, Tipton burst into laughter, then leisurely strolled from the room.

Carl stood rooted to the spot, seething with anger as he listened to him continue laughing as he walked down the hall.

"One of these days you'll get yours Tipton. And I sure hope I'm there to see it!" Carl mumbled under his breath.

He harms himself who does harm to another,
and the evil plan is most harmful to the planner.

— Hesiod

Chapter Eleven

Reluctantly and after a great deal of protest, Noah, along with Tommy, agreed to go with Ida. But before they left, Ida made sure Sarah had taken two of the sedatives Ben had given her and was comfortably resting in bed.

As they drove back into town, Ida said, "First we'll stop at the cafe and get you boys somethin' to eat. Have either of you had anything to eat today?"

"Nope." Tommy replied.

"You poor things. You must be starvin' by now. Well don't you worry I'll fix you right up!"

"Thank you Ma'am." Tommy said as he glanced sideways at Noah for approval.

Noah was unresponsive and quietly continued to glower out the window.

"What about you Noah? You hungry?" Ida asked, more to engage him in conversation than anything else. She knew he must be starving.

"No." Noah replied solemnly. And the remainder of the drive was spent in silence.

As they neared the cafe, Ida was relieved to see there weren't many cars parked out front. Although it was in between the lunch and dinner crowd, there were days when the cafe would see a steady stream of customers from open to close. Ida was glad this wasn't one of them, however, she still pulled around back to avoid anyone seeing them.

"You two just sit tight for a minute."

Ida then got out of the car and hurried inside.

"Walter?" she called as she placed her keys on the pegboard next to the door.

"Right here Miz Ida," Walter replied as he quickly put down his spatula and walked around the stove toward his boss.

"Listen Walt, I've got Sarah's boys outside and they look pretty bad. I'm tellin' you this because I don't want you to make any comment or act like you notice at all. Understand?"

"Yes Ma'am."

"Any meatloaf and potatoes left from lunch?"

"Plenty."

"Good. Clear off part of the counter over there and set two plates with meatloaf, gravy, some mashed potatoes and carrots. Any biscuits left?"

"Yep."

"Give them some of those also. Oh and two large glasses of milk. I'll be right back."

As Ida shuffled Noah and Tommy inside, Walter was just setting their full plates down while Sam placed a couple of stools in front of the counter.

"Hey boys, hope you're hungry!" Walter said lightly, trying not to stare. The left side of Noah's face was covered with a purple and black bruise, and his left eye was completely swollen shut. Tommy had fingerprint bruises up and down the length of his neck that were visible even at a distance.

As the two sat down, Tommy's stomach growled appreciatively and he looked up at Noah for a que to begin eating.

When Noah made no attempt to pick up his fork, Ida said, "What's the matter? You don't like meatloaf?"

Without lifting his head, Noah replied, "Yes Ma'am, I do. I'm just not hungry."

"Noah, you have to eat somethin' and so does Tommy, and it looks like he's not gonna eat until you do. So if you won't eat for yourself, then do it for him."

"Go ahead Li'l Bit, eat."

Tommy picked up his fork and began to gobble up his meal so fast Ida was afraid he might choke.

"Slow down there shorty, there's plenty more where that came from."

When several minutes passed and Noah still hadn't touched his food, Ida said coaxingly, "Come on Noah just try it. If you don't like it, we can make you somethin' else."

"No thank you Ma'am. I'm not hungry."

"All right then, how about a piece of Walter's famous cherry pie? Or double layer chocolate cake?"

Noah shook his head in the negative.

Ida was happy to see at least Tommy's appetite had not been affected by the morning's tragedy. At the mention of chocolate cake, his eyes lit up and he said, "You've got chocolate cake?"

"You bet I do! And I believe I have a piece with your name on it if you finish what's in front of you."

Not for the first time today, Ida felt a twinge of pity for the McAllisters. She realized chocolate cake must be an extremely rare, if ever treat, considering their financial situation.

It took Tommy less than ten minutes to devour everything on his plate. After gulping down the last of his milk, he wiped his mouth with the back of his hand and said excitedly, "Miz Anderson, may I have my cake now?"

"Comin' right up young sir! Noah you sure you won't have a piece?"

Again, Noah shook his head no.

While Tommy polished off his dessert, Ida had Sam make up a box of food for them to take home, including a pie and several generous portions of chocolate cake.

"Okay fellas, go on out to the car, I'll be there in a minute," Ida said, as Tommy drank the last of his second glass of milk.

Ida waited for the door to close behind them before she said to Walter and Sam, "I'm takin' them over to Doc Hadley's, I'm not sure when I'll be back, but if Sheriff Tipton comes by lookin' for them, try to stall him here as long as you can. Tell him you think I took them back to my place. Just tryin' to find us should keep him out of trouble for a little while anyway."

"Miz Ida what's goin' on here? And what the heck happened out there last night? Those kids look like they've had the snot beat out of them and then some!"

"I know they do Walt, but just remember things aren't always what they seem, so keep a lid on this would ya? I'll fill you in later."

"You got it Miz Ida."

As she pulled out of the alley, Ida looked in the rearview mirror at Noah and Tommy and said, "We're gonna stop by Doc Hadley's house first."

Noah's head jerked up violently, and as he glared back at Ida in the mirror, he fairly shouted, "Why?"

Startled by his strong reaction, she said, "Well, Ben wants to make sure you two are all right that's all."

"Miz Anderson we're fine. I don't want to go to Dr. Hadley's. Why can't we just go home now?"

"Noah, I promise I'll take you home as soon as we're through at Ben's, okay?"

Ida had no idea what had invoked such a vehement response. So she assumed it must be his desire to get back to his mother. But there was more to it than that.

Dr. Hadley's house was the last place on earth Noah wanted to go today, because that's where the beautiful Hannah Hadley lived. Noah had lost his heart to the doctor's daughter in the sixth grade.

He would never forget the moment they met for as long as he lived. It happened one day at recess as he and Curtis were playing tetherball. Neither had noticed the two fifth grade girls, Hannah and her friend, Lily, playing on the next tetherball mound until one of them started crying hysterically.

Both boys rushed to see what had happened and found Hannah had somehow gotten her long, dark hair, tightly entwined in the tetherball chain.

As Lily and Curtis looked on, Noah sprang into action. Mumbling soothing words of comfort, he began to untangle her hair.

While he worked, the fresh scent of magnolias filled his nostrils. From that moment on he would forever associate magnolias with Hannah Hadley.

Once she was free, she looked up to thank her rescuer, and as their eyes met, a jolt of electricity pierced Noah's heart. Her large, beautiful blue eyes, fringed with long black lashes were still brimming with tears, and Noah had to fight an incredible urge to wipe them away.

For several moments he simply stood motionless, quietly mesmerized by her beauty. Then the bell suddenly rang and both girls turned and ran to get in line.

It wasn't until Curtis slapped him on the back and said, "C'mon or we're gonna be late," that Noah realized he was still staring after her.

From then on, Noah looked for her on the playground at every recess, though he was never bold enough to approach her.

Since starting high school this year, he rarely saw her because they no longer attended the same school.

Now as they pulled up in front of the Hadley home, Noah's heart began to pound wildly in his chest. He was certain that any second he was going to vomit.

As Ida knocked on the door and the three of them stood waiting for Hannah to arrive, Noah wondered how much worse this day could possibly get.

It didn't take long to get an answer. The look of horror on Hannah's face as she opened the door to them, made Noah want to turn on his heals and run away as fast as he could.

"Gosh, Noah, what happened to your face?" Hannah gasped, shocked by his appearance.

Noah mumbled something about falling as he shuffled past her into the house.

Much to his dismay, Hannah had only gotten lovelier since the last time he saw her. She was tall and slender, and her silky, long, dark brown hair still smelled of freshly cut magnolias, he noticed as he passed in front of her. And in that moment he wished fervently for a hole to open in the floor and swallow him.

"Is your daddy still at Farley's, Hannah?" Ida asked.

"No Ma'am. Somethin' happened to one of Mr. Spencer's farm hands, and Daddy had to go tend to him. He stopped by here first though and said you'd be by and he told me to ask you to stay here until he got back."

Alarmed, Ida asked, "Was Sheriff Tipton with him?"

"I don't think so Miz Anderson."

"How long ago was that?"

"Hmm, maybe forty-five minutes to an hour."

It would have taken Tipton only twenty minutes or so to reach the McAllister farm, Ida calculated. Knowing what perverse pleasure the bully took in harassing and tormenting the weak and unprotected, Ida feared greatly for her friend's safety, for she was certain Ernest would have headed there straightaway after leaving Ben.

"Listen kids, I need to run an errand, I won't be gone long and I want you to stay put and wait for Dr. Hadley, understand?" Ida said, not really expecting a reply as she walked quickly to the door.

Her mind was already racing toward what to do next, pick up Walter or Sam to go with her to Sarah's — or not waste the precious time and go alone.

Fortunately, Ben pulled up in front of the house before she even reached her car, much to Ida's overwhelming relief.

"Boy, Ben, am I glad to see you. I was just headed for Sarah's. C'mon, get in."

"All right just let me get changed, it'll only take me a minute."

"I'll head on over and meet you out there then," Ida said, not sure she could explain even to Ben, the sense of urgency she felt.

"Hold on there Ida, you're not going out there alone. I won't take more than a minute, I promise."

As Ben stepped away from his car, Ida could see he was pretty well covered with blood. Feeling a little sheepish for her lack of concern for anyone but Sarah, she asked, "Is Jesse's farm hand okay?"

"It was Erin Iverson, and yeah, he'll make it, not sure how much use he'll have in that arm though. It's a real shame, he's got a young wife and baby to support." Ben said as he hurried for the door.

Noah, Tommy, and Hannah, stood right where they had been when Ida left the house only moments ago. Ben paused in front of the them just long enough to briefly look over the boys, then say to his daughter, "Hannah, get some ice and wrap it in a dish towel for Noah to put on his face."

To Noah he said, "It'll help the swelling go down, son."

Addressing Tommy now, he continued, "What about you young man? You doin' okay?"

"Yes sir, I'm fine."

"Good. Listen, Miz Anderson and I have something to take care of. We won't be gone long so just stay put 'til we get back," Ben said, then began to unbutton his shirt as he started down the hallway to change his clothes.

The belief in a supernatural source of evil is not necessary; men alone are quite capable of every wickedness.

— Joseph Conrad

Chapter Twelve

Sheriff Tipton wasted no time in heading for the McAllisters. And as he drove, it was all he could do not to laugh out loud at his good fortune. Noble McAllister had been a thorn in his side for far too long. And in recent months, it had felt more like a knife than a thorn. McAllister had been threatening to go to the Atlanta authorities and expose the truth about those murdered drifters. Dead so long now, Ernest could hardly recall their faces. Why he couldn't put it behind him like everyone else had done was beyond Tipton's ability to fathom.

Well it sure doesn't matter now, Ernest thought, chuckling out loud in spite of himself. He also had to smile at the fact, that no one would ever know he had actually been plotting Noble's demise for the last several weeks. Waiting for just the right moment and opportunity to end the drunkard's life in such a way no one would ever suspect foul play.

Now that the fickle hand of fate had relieved him of that task, Tipton suddenly felt disappointed, almost cheated, in fact. However, that emotion didn't last long as the sheriff's mind took off in another direction. Now that Noble was out of the way, there was nothing stopping him from going after that little punk, Noah. He had not forgotten what that boy had done to his Billy several years back, and if the truth be told, he also blamed the little snot for his wife, Ruby, leaving.

Switching direction again, Tipton's thoughts drifted back to that day.

By the time Billy and he returned home from the McAllisters, his sour mood had escalated into rage. When the timid Ruby had had the nerve to suggest that maybe their son was equally at fault, Ernest had lost his temper entirely. He slapped the fragile woman across the face so hard she fell to the ground. Pulling her up by her hair he warned her about smarting off, then shoved her hard toward the kitchen and shouted after her to get dinner on, followed by a string of foul expletives that, as it always did, cut through her heart like a knife.

For Ruby Tipton, that was the final straw in a long history of abuse she had suffered at the hands of her husband. The next morning, she, along with a few meager possessions, were gone, never to be seen or heard from again, despite Ernest's attempts to locate her.

Before Tipton's mind could wander further, he was at the McAllisters. He got out of the squad car and stood with his hands on his hips for several moments, surveying his surroundings. It had been a long time since he had been there, and the place had only fallen deeper into disrepair over the years.

Tipton lifted his hat from his head and with the back of his arm, wiped the sweat from his brow. He walked across the yard and to the porch, hesitating only a moment as a euphoric since of excitement began to build in his chest.

Whoever said revenge was a dish best served cold, sure knew what they were talkin' about, he thought, as a diabolical smile slithered across his features. Then he continued up the stairs to the front door.

Tipton opened the screen door and knocked loudly.

When no one answered, he pounded a little harder and called out, "Mrs. McAllister, Sheriff Tipton here. Open up, I need to speak with you and your boys."

Ernest allowed only a few more seconds to pass, then turned the knob and pushed the door open, stepped over the threshold and cautiously entered the house. At first he thought no one was home, then he heard the creaking of mattress springs somewhere toward the back of the house.

With his senses on high alert, he walked to the edge of the living room, cocked his head to one side and listened. He thought he heard faint, but steady breathing coming from one of the rooms.

In rapid succession, a series of mental images raced through Tipton's head. In his mind's eye, Noah McAllister burst from the back bedroom and charged toward him. Having no recourse, he pulled his gun from its holster and discharged a lethal shot straight into Noah's chest, dropping the boy in mid-stride. Clear case of self-defense.

Tipton grinned maliciously and his entire body began to tingle with anticipation at the confrontation he hoped would come.

"This day just keeps gettin' better and better," he whispered under his breath. Then he slowly unsnapped the holster strap and drew his pistol. Stealthily making his way down the hall, checking first the bathroom to the right of him, then the bedroom to his left.

He took notice of the copious amount of blood on the floor from Noble's arm the night before, mentally filed it away, closed the door behind him, and continued on toward the last bedroom at the end of the hall. The door was slightly ajar so Tipton peered through the crack.

Ernest was stunned by the site of Sarah McAllister asleep in bed. He watched her for several moments, then slowly, quietly, pushed the door open a little farther to get a better look into the room.

Suddenly remembering Ben's comments about the sedatives, the scene before him began to make sense. It occurred to him that Ida must have taken the boys with her so Sarah could rest.

Still wary, he pushed the door open even wider, and quickly scanned the room. When he was confident they were alone, he holstered his gun and soundlessly approached the bed.

As he stared down at Sarah's sleeping form, his pulse began to quicken. It had been a long time since he'd even touched a woman, and never one as lovely as Sarah McAllister.

One tantalizingly creamy, white, breast, was partially exposed to his view, and his arousal was instantaneous. Almost painful in its suddenness. With labored breathing, Ernest reached out to touch the taunting flesh. As his body shook with pent up desire, he was at once torn between an intense need to violently, brutally, satisfy himself, and something else, something he couldn't articulate. Fleetingly, he wondered what passion would look like in her eyes.

Kneeling beside the bed, he began to slowly unbutton Sarah's blouse. When she didn't stir, he was emboldened to slide her bra strap gently down her arm just enough to completely release one breast from its confinement.

With a touch as light as a feather, Ernest ran the back of his hand across her nipple, provoking an immediate, if unconscious response. Nearly overcome with lust, he bent his head and began planting soft kisses down her neck and shoulder. Then, as he began to kneed the breast still nestled in her bra, he took the exposed nipple between his teeth and began to tease it with his tongue.

Sarah moaned softly, causing Ernest to stop momentarily, then, encouraged by her lack of resistance, he grew more forceful.

As Sarah began to rouse from her drug induced sleep, yet still lingering in that foggy state of half aware, she thought the gentle hands caressing her body so hungrily now were Noble's. In that near dream state, and with an overwhelming sense of relief, it was easy to accept that the past twenty-four hours had been nothing but a bad dream. A nightmare from which she was about to awake.

Wanting desperately to believe that, Sarah sighed seductively, and gave in to the pleasurable sensations building within her. With her eyes still closed, she smiled, and reached out to touch her husband's body, a body she knew nearly as well as she knew her own. As soon as her hands made contact, she realized something was wrong, and in that instant, all residual effects of the sedatives evaporated as she became horrifyingly aware that the man on top of her wasn't Noble.

Suddenly, her eyes flew open, and at the sight of Ernest looming above her, Sarah began to scream. Tipton's reaction was to clamp a bruising, suffocating hand across her mouth to silence her.

Any illusion he may have had of her welcoming his advances, vanished when he saw the look in her terrified eyes. In that same moment, he became consumed with blind rage toward, not only Sarah, but every other woman in his life, including Ruby, he felt had rejected or thwarted him in some way.

Releasing his hand from her mouth, Tipton smiled slyly and said, "Go ahead, scream as loud as you want, because there's no one around to hear you, is there?"

One word reverberated in Sarah's mind, and she cried out, "Why?"

With a cruel laugh, Ernest arrogantly replied, "Because I can."

Then he bent his head close to her ear and whispered, "Relax Sarah, you might even enjoy bein' with a man whose not too drunk to satisfy you."

At Tipton's mention of Noble, Sarah became enraged. Without warning, she began to wildly buck and twist beneath him.

Catching him off guard by the unexpectedness of her gyrations, she was able to throw him off of her. In one fluid motion, she rolled from the bed to the floor and began to crawl toward the door.

Unfortunately, Tipton was on top of her in a matter of seconds. He grabbed her roughly by the hair and pulled her to her feet, drew back his hand and slapped her so hard across the face, blood shot from her nose, spraying in all directions. The blow temporarily stunned her into submission.

Picking her up by her shoulders as though she were weightless, he slammed her against the wall. Then he stepped back several feet and began to unbuckle the belt which held his holstered gun. He tossed it haphazardly onto the bed and started to unbuckle the belt holding up his pants, as he did, he smiled at Sarah wickedly and said, "I'm gonna enjoy this. Yes sir, I'm gonna enjoy teachin' you this lesson on how to respect a man."

Sarah felt paralyzed, and could do nothing but look on helplessly as she slid down the wall. Every bone, muscle, and organ she had, exploded in excruciating pain as her body impacted with the unyielding surface.

As blackness began to close in around her, one simple thought entered her mind, So this is what it feels like to die.

Suddenly, she felt neither fear nor pain, just a quiet sense of calming peace. Yet, as soon as she closed her eyes in acceptance, an image of Noah and Tommy sprang into view.

My babies! her mind screamed, and on the heels of that thought, she was struck by a ferocious desire to live. Immediately, she began to struggle back to full consciousness, and when she finally opened her eyes, it was just in time to see Tipton coming at her with his arm raised, about to strike her with his belt.

Sarah threw up her hands to protect her face, thereby taking the brunt of the assault across her forearms. As Ernest drew back to inflict another blow, she pulled her knees in close to her chest, braced herself against the wall, and with the speed of an angry, venomous snake, shot her legs out in front of her, catching Tipton at the knees. Then she raked her heels down his shins, quickly rolled to one side and got to her feet.

Ernest screamed in agony, let go of the belt, and bent over to grab his throbbing knees. Without a moments hesitation, Sarah picked up the ceramic lamp from the nightstand and, with all the strength she could muster, cracked it over his head.

Tipton dropped like a rock, though he was still conscious. So before he could recover completely, she swung the broken lamp at him again, and this time knocked him out cold.

Then she threw the lamp aside, fell on top of her attacker, straddled his waist, put her hands to his throat and began to squeeze until her hands shook.

Every great mistake has a halfway moment,
a split second when it can be recalled and perhaps remedied.

— Pearl Buck

Chapter Thirteen

"Hurry Ben. No tellin' what that no good Tipton is doin' out there!" Ida said nervously.

Stepping on the gas a little harder, Ben replied, "Take it easy Ida, Tipton's stupid, I'll give you that, but even he's not stupid enough to really harm Mrs. McAllister."

"So say you, but I know better. Tipton's capable of a lot worse than you give him credit for."

"What makes you say that?"

Feeling as though she had said too much, Ida replied, "Never mind, I'm just talkin' nonsense that's all. Pay no attention to this ol' woman. I'm sure you're right."

After a short pause in the conversation, Ben said, "Ida, why do I get the feeling you haven't told me the whole story? What is it you know about Tipton that I don't? And exactly what was that "bad blood" between Noble and Ernest you referred to this morning?"

"I've told you everything that happened out at the McAllister farm last night as Sarah told it to me, Ben."

"No, I mean before. What happened to cause that rift between Ernest and Noble McAllister?"

"You know, it was a long time ago, and now that Noble's dead, I'd say it's not important anymore. Best to let sleeping dogs lie."

"I think it is important. I know it goes all the way back to the deaths of Edna and Harvey ... and those drifters."

Taken aback, Ida said, "What are you talkin' about Ben?"

"Don't look so shocked. It's just that I don't believe those drifters ever made it out of town ... did they?"

"What makes you think I'd know?"

"Well, for one thing, you know everything that goes on around here — nothing gets by you. Two, Walter and Sam were part of that mob that went out searching that night, and if something had happened, they would have told you. Am I right?"

Before answering his question, Ida asked, "What makes you think they didn't get away?"

"Interestingly enough, I've stayed in contact with one of the investigators through the years, Mike Halverson. And the funny thing is, despite their best efforts, they have yet to uncover any trace of those people. It's like they vanished from the face of the earth. Don't you find that odd? Wouldn't you think somebody, somewhere, in some other town would have come in contact with them?"

Ida felt a cold chill run down her spine. "Oh Ben, some things are best left alone, and this is truly one of them. And if you're so sure I know what happened, why haven't you asked me about it before?"

"Because, up until now, I wasn't sure I wanted to know the truth. After all, some of those men I believe were involved, are my friends and neighbors also."

"Why now?"

"If I'm going to help Mrs. McAllister and her family, I need to know what it is I'm dealing with here. And exactly what you know Tipton is capable of."

Realizing that if Ben was going to stick his neck out for Sarah and her boys, he had a right to know the truth, most of it anyway, Ida said, "Murder. Ernest Tipton is capable of murder. You were right about those drifters, they never made it too far out of town.

"The long and short of it is this -— when they caught up with that couple that night and found them with some of Harvey and Edna's belongings, things went nuts, and Tipton shot and killed the girl. Now, the way I heard it, was that his gun went off accidentally, but he did it nonetheless. When the gun went off, the man with her tried to make a run for it, that's when nearly everyone there got involved and beat him to death. Again, the way I heard it, was that it was all Ernest's idea to cover it up.

"I was told that Noble McAllister was there as well, and was the only one who tried to stop it. Nearly got the snot beat out off him for his trouble, so I was told.

"Anyway, that's where the bad blood between them started. And now that you know what I know — what are you gonna do with it?" Ida finished matter-of-factly. She deliberately failed to mention Leonard and Missy by name, fearing Ben might suspect she knew more about them than she was willing to admit.

"Nothing, except use it against Ernest if I can. What did they do with the bodies?"

"I don't know."

"Yes you do."

"Well, that's all I'm gonna tell you."

"You're a tough old bird! That's what I like about you."

"We've been friends a long time, Ben. I really hope you don't make me regret trustin' you with information that could hurt a lot of good people."

"Don't worry Ida, I was always sure the truth was something like that, and I've never said a word to Mike. And I doubt I ever will, unless there was a way to make Tipton and Tipton alone culpable."

"Good."

Moments later, Ben and Ida pulled up behind Tipton's squad car. Upon hearing a raised voice coming from inside the house, they both jumped out of the car and bolted for the porch, up the few steps and to the door, which was wide open.

Ben entered the house first and headed straight for the back bedroom where he could hear Sarah screaming, "Ernest Tipton you are NEVER gonna hurt my family again! NOT ... EVER ... EVER ... AGAIN! YOU HEAR ME?"

As Ben rushed into the room he was stopped dead in his tracks by what he saw. Ida, who was not far behind, gasped audibly as she came up beside the doctor. The two simultaneously looked at one another, shocked and speechless. Of all the scenarios either had envisioned they'd find when they got to the McAllister farm, this was not one of them.

Hadley was the first to recover and quickly grabbed Sarah around the waist and tried to pull her off the unconscious Tipton. For such a small woman, Sarah, at least at that moment, seemed to have phenomenal strength. It took Ben several forceful yanks before he was able to pry her away from the sheriff.

Still crying hysterically, Sarah continued to flail and thrash about as Ben held her awkwardly in his arms, several feet above the ground.

"Sarah! Sarah, honey! It's okay, it's okay. Stop! It's just me, Ida, and Dr. Hadley, Ben Hadley."

Suddenly, Sarah became still. She stared at Ida as though she didn't recognize her, then slumped over, put her hands to her face and began to cry softly.

Ida put her arms around the sobbing woman and said soothingly, "Shh, shhh. It's okay honey, we're here now."

Ben gently set Sarah down on the bed as Ida continued to hold her in her arms. After a few moments, Sarah lifted her face to Ida, then looked over to where Ernest lay motionless, and cried, "Oh Miz Ida, I think I might've killed Mr. Tipton!"

"Ben?"

The doctor walked over to the inert body of Dawson's sheriff, knelt beside him and took his pulse, which, much to his relief was strong and steady.

"He's fine. He'll come around in a few minutes. Though I'm happy to say, by the looks of that egg-sized lump on his forehead, he's going to have a headache the size of Texas when he does."

As Ben was talking, Ida found Sarah's tattered robe and wrapped it around her partially clothed friend, whose blouse had been nearly torn off in the scuffle.

Ben stood up, looked around the room for something to tie up Tipton with, and spotted his gunbelt on the bed. After putting the sheriff in his own handcuffs, Ben removed all of the bullets from his gun and put them in his pocket, then put the gun back into its holster.

To Ida, Ben said, "Can you get my bag from the car."

"Sure."

Kneeling in front of Sarah, he asked, "Mrs. McAllister, are you okay?"

When Sarah nodded, Ben continued, "What happened here?"

"I ... I don't know. I just ... I woke up and he was on top of me ... and ..."

"Did he r ...?"

Sarah's face turned seven shades of red. Squeezing her eyes shut tightly, she vigorously shook her head "no" before Ben could finish his sentence.

"It's all right. This isn't your fault you know."

"I know, it's just ..." she couldn't bear to think about how she had felt, at least for those few brief moments before she knew it was Tipton touching her. Though it had been less than twenty-four hours since his death, and life with Noble had been a misery for many years, Sarah suddenly missed him so much her heart ached.

Much to her relief, Ida cut off any further explanation as she hurried back into the room, handed the bag to Hadley, and said, "Here you go Ben."

After cleaning the blood from Sarah's face, and tending to some minor cuts and scrapes, Ben was satisfied that other than some serious bruising, she was otherwise going to be okay.

Just as he finished with Sarah, Ernest began to moan, so Ben walked over to him, nudged him roughly with his foot and said, "Wake up! Wake up you sorry sack of crap!"

It took Ernest several moments before he was fully able to open his eyes. When he did, an unbearable pain shot through his head. When he reached up and touched the knot on his forehead, he winced and said, "What the heck?"

Then he rolled to his side and with his cuffed hands pushed himself into a sitting position.

"You have a lot to answer for Tipton!" Ben said angrily.

"What're you talkin' about?" Ernest replied gruffly, as he rubbed the back of his head.

"I'm talking about what you've done here! I'm talking about attempted rape!"

"Hold on there Doc! You got it all wrong! She attacked me! All I did was come out here to do my duty as sheriff and ask some legitimate questions about what happened to Noble. Next thing you know, this little hellcat comes at me with a lamp!" Glaring at Sarah now, Tipton continued, "I call that attempted murder!"

If the situation weren't so serious, Ben would have laughed in Ernest's face at the absurd accusation. "You're a liar! And really Ernest, is that the way you want to go with this?"

"That's the way it is! Now get me outta these handcuffs!"

"Listen you, I'm not sure who it is you intend to peddle that story to, but it's not gonna wash. And I would suggest, before you dig yourself any deeper into that hole, you think long and hard on it."

"Oh yeah, what if I told you I can prove Noble McAllister was murdered?"

"What?" Ben threw back at him sarcastically.

"That's right! I can prove it."

"No you can't — because it didn't happen!"

All the while Ben and Ernest were arguing, Ida's mind was in overdrive. She would love to see Tipton severely punished for what he had done to Sarah. However, even though she knew he was bluffing about having any proof whatsoever of a crime that had never been committed, she also realized that to an outside party, things might not look so cut and dried.

Wary of drawing any more people into the situation, Ida said, "Can I talk to you for a minute Ben?"

Ben glared down at Tipton without blinking, then turned and walked over to the bed where Ida and Sarah were sitting.

Ida motioned for him to come in closer, so he knelt in front of them to hear Ida whisper, "Ben, maybe for Sarah and her family's sake, we can find a compromise here.

"What if Sarah would be willin' to drop any charges against Ernest. And in exchange, he agrees to leave this family in peace to bury their dead and move on with their lives. What do you think?"

"Ida, you're not serious? We finally have an opportunity to rid this town of that buffoon, and you — you of all people want to find a compromise that would allow him to stay?"

"Now Ben, you know I'd love nothin' more than to get rid of that rat. But really, I see it sort of like cuttin' our noses off to spite our faces here. If Sarah pushes Ernest, he's gonna push back, and while I know

Ernest can't prove a thing, he can cause some trouble for Sarah and her boys. Trouble they don't need. Trouble this town doesn't need."

Ben shook his head in disgust. Looking at Sarah, he said, "Well, Mrs. McAllister, we've yet to hear from you. How do you feel about letting the man who just tried to rape you, maybe even kill you, walk away as though nothing happened?"

"Dr. Hadley, I appreciate all your help, really I do. But the thing is, I just want this all to be over. I want my boys home so we can begin to try to make sense of what's happened to us, and figure out where we go from here. If that means I have to let Sheriff Tipton off the hook to get that, I don't see it as such a big price to pay."

Once again, Ben shook his head, bewildered by these two women who were so willing to let Ernest Tipton weasel his way out of this. On the other hand, Ben realized he shouldn't be surprised, weaseling his way out of sticky situations was what Tipton excelled at. Still, it rankled Ben to no end, that Ernest was going to get out of this so easily. Under his breath he vowed that somehow, someday, Ernest Tipton would get exactly was coming to him.

Courage is fear that has said its prayers.

— Dorothy Bernard

Chapter Fourteen

Grudgingly, Ernest had agreed to the offer that was made to him. Though much to Ben's astonishment, Tipton put up quite an argument, and even to the very end would not admit he had done anything wrong.

So infuriated was Ben, that as Tipton started to leave, he couldn't resist a parting shot.

Remembering the bullets in his pocket, he pulled them out, held them in the palm of his hand, and said, "By the way Tipton, I took the liberty of removing these from your gun. I wanted to make sure you didn't shoot someone else ... "accidentally"."

At the shocked expression on everyone's faces, Ben instantly regretted the taunt, and contritely finished with, "You won't be getting these back."

Tipton glared at Ben for several tense seconds, opened his mouth as though he were going to say something, thought better of it, then turned on his heel and stormed out of the house. Neither Sarah nor Ida commented on the doctor's remarks, though Ben read the rebuke clear enough in Ida's eyes.

Once Tipton was gone, Ida looked at Sarah critically and said, "Honey are you sure you're all right?" When Sarah nodded that she was, Ida continued, "Okay then. Have you had anything to eat today?"

"No. But I'm not hungry Miz Ida."

"Well, how about I fix you a cold glass of tea?"

"I'm sorry, I don't have any tea, but some water would be nice."

"Comin' right up."

As Ida looked through Sarah's cabinets for a glass, she was horrified to discover the McAllisters had very little food in their cupboards, and even less in the refrigerator. As one of the wealthier citizens of Dawson, Ida had more than enough to share, and would have gladly given her younger friend whatever she needed. However, she knew Sarah would never accept a handout, and under any other circumstances Ida would have admired her for that. This was different, so Ida vowed one way or another she was going to help this poor family, rather Sarah liked it or not.

Ida returned to the living room with the glass of water in time to catch the tail end of Ben's condolences for the loss of Noble, and, more recently, the attack from Tipton. "... and Mrs. McAllister, I'll do what I can to insure Tipton leaves you and your children alone for good."

"Thank you Dr. Hadley."

When Ida handed her the glass of water, Sarah said, "Miz Ida, where are my boys?"

"Ben and I are gonna get them and bring them home right now. You gonna be okay here alone?"

"Yeah, I'll be fine, thanks. But please hurry, I need them home."

Ida searched Sarah's face, then said encouragingly, "Sarah, you and your boys really are gonna be okay. I promise."

Sarah grabbed the older woman and held on tightly. Then she whispered in her ear, "I don't know what I did to deserve a friend like you Miz Ida. You've been such a blessing to me. Thank you."

"Oh, now. Don't get mushy on me," Ida said, her voice cracking with emotion.

As Ben and Ida headed back into town, Ida said, "Ben, there was hardly anything to eat in that house."

"How do you know? Were you snooping?"

At the indignant, outraged expression contorting Ida's face, Ben started to chuckle and said, "Take it easy Ida, I was just kidding."

"Ben Hadley, this is no laughin' matter! This family's in trouble and they need our help. Now what are we gonna do?"

Ben's smile vanished, and, feeling very much like a child that had just been reprimanded by his mother, replied, "You're right Ida, I'm sorry. I was just trying to lighten things up a little, that's all. Of course we're going to help."

"Well, all right then. Sorry I yelled at you — and no I wasn't snoopin'! I was lookin' for a glass for Sarah's water."

Mumbling now, Ida continued, "It's not my fault I had to search through every cabinet and the refrigerator to find it." Then she smiled sheepishly at Ben who returned the grin with an "I knew it" smirk on his face.

Becoming serious again, Ida said, "Sarah's a proud woman Ben, she's not likely to take a hand-out from us."

"Even if it means her children will go hungry?"

"Oh, temporarily she will, in fact, I've already made up a box of food for Noah and Tommy to take home with them. But I mean over the long term. Sarah will not continue to accept our charity."

"Any ideas?"

"Yeah, one. I was thinkin' that maybe I could use Noah around the diner in the afternoons. Maybe have him sweep out front every day, that sort of thing. And I was thinkin' you could do the same. It won't be much, but I believe it'll help, and anything's better than nothin'. I'm pretty sure I'm about the only one left buyin' chickens from them, but maybe that'll change now that Noble's gone."

Ida paused, then continued, "God rest his soul. You know Ben, before the drink, Noble McAllister was a good man. Everyone liked him. Remember?"

"I do. Sad isn't it? If anyone's life should have been ruined by what happened all those years ago, it should have been Tipton's. He's the one that deserved it most. Just doesn't seem fair does it?"

"Well, God has his reasons."

"I suppose. But you know something Ida, we shouldn't have let him off so easily here. Truthfully? I don't think Ernest has any intentions of leaving the McAllisters alone. I think in the long run, we've just made things worse, now instead of overtly harassing them, he'll find sneakier ways to torment that family.

147

But I meant what I said to Mrs. McAllister, I'll do whatever I can to prevent him from causing them any more grief."

After Ben and Ida left, Sarah returned her empty glass to the sink, then sat down at the table, put her hands to her face and cried. For perhaps ten minutes she allowed herself to wallow in self pity. When she felt there wasn't another tear left to shed, she sat up straight, bowed her head, folded her hands, and began to pray.

Prayer had always sustained and fortified her through the worst times in her life, and this time was no different. By the time Sarah finished with, "in Jesus' name, Amen," and rose from the table, she felt measurably better knowing that she and her boys would get through this latest trial. There was no doubt left in her mind God would see to that.

A short time later, she stood in the doorway to the bedroom, surveying the damage. Shards from the broken lamp littered the floor, along with splatters of her blood. At the reminder, she gingerly touched her nose, then winced in pain.

Unbidden, images of her struggle with Tipton filled her mind, so Sarah squeezed her eyes tightly shut to clear them from her head, and was instantly assaulted by an unpleasant smell. Realizing the sour, sweaty odor was from Tipton, Sarah suddenly felt ill and rushed to the bathroom. She made it to the toilet just in time to release the pent up bile in her throat.

She quickly stripped off her clothes, got into the shower and as hot water began to pour over her, she vigorously scrubbed every inch of her contaminated skin until it was raw.

After she was through with her shower, Sarah attacked the bedroom with the same frenzied vengeance as she had her body. She stripped the bed of its linens, and scoured the floor with ammonia. Afterward, though she could hardly afford to lose them, she took the sheets, along with the clothes she had worn earlier, out to the burn barrel and in a matter of minutes, reduced them to ashes.

Feeling much better, Sarah went back inside and began cleaning the rest of the house. When she got to Noah and Tommy's room, she lingered at the closed door with a fresh bucket of ammonia water. Steeling herself, she grabbed the knob, turned it slowly and deliberately, then forcefully pushed open the door.

Her eyes were immediately drawn to the puddle of blood on the floor, Noble's blood. She closed her eyes against the tears that threatened to spill down her cheeks. Then, forcing a resolve she in no way felt, she walked over to the spot, reached into the bucket and pulled out the sopping wet cleaning rag and dropped it on top of the stain.

As she painstakingly scrubbed every inch of the floor, a myriad of memories flooded back to her. An image of a handsome, young Noble on their wedding night, brought a whisper of a smile to her face. They had been so in love, and so inexperienced at lovemaking, that even years later at the mere mention of that night, their faces would turn beet red, and neither could control their laughter.

Another memory just as precious popped into Sarah's head. It was of the first time Noble had held his son. Her husband's strong, calloused hands shook so badly as he reached out to take the baby from her, that Sarah feared he might drop Noah. But as soon as she pulled her hands away, Noble's became steady as a rock. After marveling over his offspring for several moments, Noble lifted his face to his wife. Tears of joy glistened on his cheeks, it was the very first time Sarah saw him cry.

Holding the baby securely in the crook of one arm, Noble had gotten down on his knees, and with his head bowed, he reached out and took Sarah's hand in his. To Sarah, Noble had never appeared more handsome, more masculine, or more lovable than when he had, in humble, prayerful, and tearful gratitude, thanked the Lord for the treasured blessing of his wife and son.

Those were the good memories, the memories she would carry in her heart until the day she died. As to what he had become over the last few years, Sarah made up her mind she would never think on it again. She would only remember the good, kind man he had been before all of their troubles started.

As she prepared to stand up, Sarah felt a warm, strong hand gently squeeze her shoulder. Startled by the intrusion, she looked up, fully expecting to find a living, breathing person behind her, that's how solidly real the touch had felt. When she found no one in the room with her, she was struck by an overpowering, and undeniable truth that Noble had just said good-bye.

Sarah whispered to the empty room, "Save me a place in heaven, my love." And for the first time in longer than she could remember, she actually felt a sense of peace.

By the time Ida got back to the farm with Noah and Tommy, the sun had nearly set. On their return to Ben's house, the doctor looked each boy over a little more thoroughly then he had earlier in the day. Only when he was satisfied that neither one had anything more seriously wrong than a swollen face, black eye, and some ugly bruising, did he allow Ida to leave with them.

Before Ida left, she and Ben agreed to get together the following day to come up with a plan to help the McAllisters. Both decided tomorrow would be soon enough to mention the job to Noah and Sarah.

When Ida pulled up in front of Sarah's, she did not shut the engine off, or get out, deciding this time was for the McAllisters alone. As Noah and Tommy got out of the car, Ida reminded Noah to take the box of food with him, then as the boys were walking to the porch she called out, "Tell your momma I'll be by tomorrow, Noah."

When Sarah heard Ida's car pull up to the house, she walked out onto the porch just in time to wave to her friend as she drove off. As Ida waved back, she stuck her head out of the window and called out, "I'll see you tomorrow."

As Sarah watched her children walk toward her, she felt a tightening in her throat at the sadness that radiated from them as they shuffled to the door.

Trying to put on a brave face and lighten the mood a little, she opened her arms as they got closer and said, "I missed you two!"

Tommy ran into his mother's arms and they hugged one another tightly. Noah, who was carrying the box, said, "We missed you too Momma," but did not return his mother's smile as he continued, with his head down, on into the house.

Once inside, Noah went into the kitchen and set the box, which was filled to the brim with food, on the table. As he was turning around, he heard Tommy suck his breath in loudly, then blurt out, "Momma! What happened to your face?" from the living room.

As Noah hurried to his mother's side, Sarah turned her face away from them and covered her cheek. She hadn't bothered to look in the mirror after showering, so she had no idea that one side of her face bore Tipton's bruising handprint, nor that her nose was slightly swollen.

"Oh, it's nothin', I'm okay," Sarah said lightly.

"Momma! Turn around!" Noah said commandingly.

Realizing she wouldn't be able to hide her face indefinitely. Sarah slowly turned toward Noah and Tommy and let her hand fall from her face. The look that came over her oldest son, chilled Sarah to the bone.

Gritting his teeth as he spoke, Noah ground out, "Who did that to you?"

"Noah, listen to me — it doesn't matter, it's done and over with, and I am gonna be fine. And you and Tommy are gonna be fine."

"Who. . .did that. . .to you?" Noah said again, even less able to conceal his anger then when he had asked the question the first time.

"Noah, please. Really son, it doesn't matter. It's over and we're just gonna forget about it."

"Momma, tell me what happened to you!"

Sarah took her son's face lovingly between her hands. Looking deep into his tortured eyes, she said, "My precious, precious boy, we've had enough sadness, and violence, and anger, and hate, and death, to last us a lifetime. And I know you feel responsible for us now, but Noah, we're in this together as a family.

If I tell you what happened, you have to promise you're not gonna do anything foolish, because it's already been dealt with.

"Promise?"

Noah stared at his mother for several moments before nodding in acquiesce.

"It was Sheriff Ernest Tipton."

The evil of the world is made possible by nothing but the sanction you give it.

— Ayn Rand

Chapter Fifteen

As Noah lay in bed staring up at the ceiling, his thoughts were focused on one thing — Sheriff Ernest Tipton!

Sarah would not give him the details of what happened. She would only say that the matter had been settled and that the sheriff had gotten the shortest end of that stick. As he had looked at his diminutive mother, with the marks from Tipton's brutish hand so clearly imprinted on her face, Noah found that hard to believe. And although he had promised he wouldn't do anything foolish, he couldn't control his mind from envisioning a number of ways to make the sheriff pay for the pain he had inflicted upon Sarah.

Finally, before drifting off into troubled sleep, Noah wondered what it was about his family that caused the Tiptons to hate them so much.

Sarah also found it difficult to sleep that night. As she lay in bed tossing and turning, one jumbled thought after another churned inside of her head. Eventually, she was able to consciously force herself to quiet her mind. And just before she too drifted off, a single thought followed her into slumber — don't forget the ring.

Tommy was not plagued by the same unrest as his mother and Noah. He had fallen fast asleep nearly as soon as his head hit the pillow. Perhaps that was a result of the resilience of youth. Or perhaps it was his unwavering faith in Noah. After all, Noah had said he would never let anything bad happen to him. For Tommy, that was a truth he never once doubted.

Sarah awoke the next morning before the sun was even up, and the first thought on her mind was of Noble's ring. She wasn't sure why that ring seemed so important all of a sudden, but it was.

It had been passed down through countless generations of McAllister men. And Sarah loved the story behind the unique piece of jewelry.

Noble had told her that the ring had begun life as a silver spoon that once belonged to the first McAllister ever to set foot on American soil. An immigrant from Ireland, Sean McAllister came to America like so many before him, with a dream of a better life in his heart and nothing in his pockets save for that silver spoon.

The utensil was of no real value to anyone but Sean. It had belonged to his older, much loved sister, and only living relative, Siobhan. She had given it to him as an afterthought, really. As he made his goodbyes to her and her husband, she had frantically looked around their tiny kitchen and spied the spoon.

Seizing it in her delicate hands, she had presented it to Sean as though it had been the crown jewels of London.

In her lilting Irish brogue, Siobhan had said in all seriousness, "Now Sean, ya listen to me dear. Take this here spoon to America with ya. Whenever ya get homesick, take it out and hold it in yer hands, and remember it comes from yer beloved Ireland."

And then the last words she had ever spoken to her bold, adventurous brother were, "Go n-éirí an bóthar leat. Go raibh an ghaoth go brách ag do chúl. Go lonraí an ghrian go te ar d'aghaidh. Go dtite an bháisteach go mín ar do pháirceanna. Agus go mbuailimid le chéile arís, Go gcoinní Dia i mbos A láimhe thú."

Noble had been able to recite the blessing in the old Gaelic language as if it were his native tongue. Though he had had to translate it for Sarah. May the road rise to meet you. May the wind be always at your back. May the sun shine warm upon your face, the rains fall soft upon your fields. And until we meet again, may God hold you in the hollow of His hand.

A few short years after arriving in America, Sean met and married Mary Francis Rafferty. Nine months to the day, Michael

Sean McAllister was born. Although Sean had improved his lot in life tenfold after coming to this new land, he never did become a man of any means. Though he would have argued that point, for he felt very rich indeed.

Upon the birth of his first son, Sean took the silver spoon and melted it down to make a silver locket for his wife, and a silver ring to pass down to his son. Into the roughly carved band, he etched the letter "M", though only the McAllister men recognized it as such.

For more than one hundred years, that McAllister family heirloom had connected father to son and so on. Now it belonged to Noah. Sarah regretted that she would not be able to teach him the Irish blessing that had also been passed down with the ring.

Sarah slipped out of bed and retrieved the box that contained the ring which had been safely tucked away in the bottom drawer of their dresser. Noble had never been able to wear it, because it had always been too small for any of his fingers.

Sarah sat back down on the edge of the bed, then opened the box, and was surprised to find the ring resting on a folded piece of crisp white paper. It had been many years since she herself had viewed the box or its contents. However, she was fairly certain the paper had only recently been placed in the box.

Hesitantly, she removed the ring and set it aside. Then she picked up the piece of paper, and as her hands shook nervously, she unfolded it. In Noble's unmistakable handwriting was the Irish blessing, written in both Gaelic and English. Noble had signed it, "Love, Pap." As she stared down at it, her eyes misted over with tears.

Before she could contemplate the implication, there was a soft tap on her door. Wiping her eyes, Sarah said, "Come in."

Noah poked his head around the door and said, just above a whisper, "Momma, are you awake?"

"Sure son. Come on in," and then, "Where's Tommy?"

"He's still asleep."

Sarah patted the spot next to her and said, "Come sit with me, I want to show you somethin.'"

After Noah was settled beside her, she picked up the ring and held it out to him.

"What is it?"

Taking a deep breath, Sarah began, "Noah, this ring belonged to your Pap, and his Pap before him." Then she went on to retell the story of the history of the silver band.

When she was finished with the recounting, she said, "And now it belongs to you."

Along with the ring, she handed him the paper with the blessing written on it.

"This is an Irish blessing, I suppose your Pap wrote it for you in case he wasn't here to recite it to you himself."

Noah took the ring and rolled it between his thumb and index finger. He stared at it intently for a moment, then handed it back to Sarah and said, "Momma, why do the Tiptons hate us so much?"

Sarah was completely caught off guard by the question. It took her several moments to recover, then several more to respond.

Speaking softly, she said, "Noah, do you remember how it really was that Tommy came to live with us?"

Noah looked at Sarah for a long time before answering.

Finally, he said, "I found him Momma. I found him on the side of the road."

Sarah felt a momentary twinge of panic. "I thought you had forgotten. You never once mentioned it."

Again Noah stared at his mother as though he were weighing his response carefully in his mind. "You told me not to tell."

Sarah gave her son a half smile and said, "That's right I did. And you were a good boy. You never talked about it with anyone did you? Not even me or your Pap. That's why I thought you had forgotten. Or maybe that was just wishful thinkin' on my part.

"Anyway, I guess you're old enough to know the truth. Although, I worry you're way too young to bear the burden of it. So are you sure you want to hear this?"

Without hesitation, Noah nodded his head.

Sighing heavily, Sarah continued, "All right then. Noah, my hope is that maybe you'll see your Pap in a different light after you know what caused him to behave the way he did." And then, "Somethin' really bad happened that day you found Tommy. Somethin' that changed your Pap, and nearly every other man in this town forever."

An hour later, Sarah concluded with, "From that day on there's been bad blood between Sheriff Tipton and our family. And it just got worse after that fight you and Billy Tipton got into."

In the retelling, Sarah had sanitized the story as much as she could without deviating from the facts.

Now that Noah knew what had changed Noble from the caring, loving man he had once been, Sarah wondered if his perception of his father would change for the better.

"Tommy doesn't know any of this, does he?"

"No. Someday, when he's old enough, I'll tell him the truth."

"Those people, are they still buried out there?"

"As far as I know."

Before any more discussion could take place, Tommy shuffled into the bedroom. Rubbing the sleep from his eyes, he said, "What time is it?"

Noah stood up and met him in the middle of the room. Ruffling his hair affectionately, he said, "Too early for a rascal like you to be up!"

"Cut it out!" Tommy replied, smiling.

Noah then continued toward the door. Without turning around, he said over his shoulder, "L'il Bit? I'm glad you're my brother."

A look of shear joy radiated across Tommy's face. He swiveled around to Noah and said with a beaming smile, "Yeah, me too."

Sarah quickly put the note, along with the ring back inside the box and held it out in front of her. As Noah reached for the knob, she said, "Noah? Don't you want to take this?"

Noah stood with his back to his mother for several moments. "No. You keep it safe for me Momma," then he left the room.

Several hours later, Dr. Ben Hadley and Ida Anderson showed up at the McAllisters. Seeing them altogether with their bruised and battered faces, made Ida cringe with pity for what they had been through. It also strengthened her resolve to help them.

As Ida, Ben, and Sarah sat down at the kitchen table, Sarah said, "Miz Ida, thank you for the box of food you gave us."

"Oh, don't mention it. It was just some stuff I had left over anyway."

"Well, thank you."

Getting right to the point, Ida said, "Sarah, Ben and I are gonna pay for Noble's funeral."

Before Sarah could argue, Ida held up her hand and continued, "Now before you say anything, we want you to know we're not offerin' you a hand out. We're offerin' you a hand up. And there's no shame at all in takin' that.

"Ben and I have worked it all out. If Noah wanted to work for us a couple of hours every afternoon, sweepin' out in front of the diner and the clinic, runnin' errands, that sort of the thing. We figured between the two of us, that would be worth about five dollars a week. Out of that, we thought we'd keep two dollars out until the cost of the funeral was paid off.

"Well, what do you think?"

Sarah squeezed her eyes shut tightly as tears of gratitude slipped down her cheeks.

Steadying her voice, she replied, "Miz Ida, Dr. Hadley, I don't know what to say. I don't know how to thank you."

"Probably best not to say anything until we hear what Noah thinks. Maybe he won't want to work for a cantankerous old bat like me," Ida said, jovially.

Noah was more than happy to accept the job, as Ida and Ben suspected he would be.

Feel not the pain of parting;
it is they who stay behind that suffer.

— Henry Wadsworth Lonfellow

Chapter Sixteen

Several weeks after Noble's funeral, just when life was beginning to settle into a not entirely unpleasant routine for the McAllister family, Noah had a run-in with Ernest Tipton.

As he was sweeping off the sidewalk in front of Ben's clinic, he saw the sheriff walking toward him out of the corner of his eye. When he was only a few feet away, Ernest loudly drew nasal mucus into his throat, then spit it on the ground in front of Noah.

Noah jerked his head up and glared at the despicable sheriff. For several seconds the two stood eye to eye, glowering at one another.

Finally, Tipton said, "Somethin' you want to say to me boy?"

Noah held his tongue but did not break eye contact.

About that time, Ben walked out onto the sidewalk.

"What's going on here?"

Without looking in the doctor's direction, Tipton said, "Not a thing Ben. Just havin' a little chat with the hired help, that's all. No law against that is there?"

Then as he walked past Noah, he said just above a whisper, "Mark my words boy, you're gonna come to no good just like your drunken daddy!"

Fiery anger flared in Noah. And it took every ounce of self-control he possessed, not to swing the broom he was squeezing in his hand at Tipton's head.

After Ernest left, Ben came up behind him and said, "You all right?"

"Yes, sir."

"Noah, don't let him get to you."

"No, sir, I won't," then he continued on with the task of cleaning the sidewalk as though nothing at all had happened.

The better Ben became acquainted with Noah, the more he liked the McAllister boy. He had a quiet dignity and strength about him that Hadley greatly admired. So when Hannah began hanging around the clinic on those afternoons she knew Noah was going to be there, the doctor had no objections.

In fact, he encouraged their blossoming friendship by inviting Noah, his family, as well as Ida, Walter, Sam, and Kitty, over for an occasional barbecue.

By the time summer turned into fall, and Hannah began her first year as a high school student, the two were inseparable.

Noah always made it a point to include Tommy in most of their activities, so that Tommy never felt left out. In fact, the three were together so often, Ida began calling them the three musketeers. Like Ben, the more she got to know Noah, the better she liked him.

The next three years were mostly a happy time for the McAllister family, yet not without strife. They continued to struggle financially, although the money Noah received from Ida and Ben helped. And Ida made sure they never went hungry. On occasion, Tipton found one lame excuse or another to harass Noah, but on the whole, even he left them pretty much alone.

It wasn't until Noah's senior year in high school that he began to see the disparity between Hannah, who was from one of the wealthiest families in town, and himself, arguably, from the poorest.

As the school year was coming to a close and Noah began contemplating life beyond high school, his future seemed pretty bleak. He would not be going off to college like Hannah would the following year. In fact, he would be lucky to find anything more than the part-time job he still maintained with Ida Anderson and Dr. Hadley.

With graduation looming less than a week away, and Tipton's comment about coming to no good weighing heavily on his heart, Noah realized there was no future for him in Dawson.

Since the war in Southeast Asia was heating up, and there was a real possibility he would be drafted anyway, Noah decided to join the Army.

He saw it not only as a way out of Dawson, but a means to provide for his mother and Tommy. There was also Hannah to consider. One day he dreamed of asking her to marry him. By joining the military he could use something called the G.I. Bill to go to college. And then maybe, if he worked really hard, he would one day be able to offer Hannah the decent life he felt she deserved.

No one was happy about his decision, least of all Hannah. But as Noah tried to explain, there was no other option available to him.

Tommy also took the news pretty hard. He idolized Noah, and could not envision a day going by without him in it. In fact, he took it so personally, that he refused to speak to Noah for days afterward.

Sarah too was heartbroken. She had cried herself to sleep the night she found out he would be leaving for Vietnam, and right into the middle of the conflict as soon as he finished bootcamp.

As Sarah helped Noah pack for his bus ride the following day, she asked, "How long do you think it'll be before we see you again?"

"I can't say for sure Momma. My tour of duty is thirteen months. But I promise I'll write every chance I get, that should make the time fly by."

Sarah turned away from her son then so he wouldn't see her tears. Noah walked up behind her and gently took hold of her shoulders then turned her around to face him.

"Momma, don't cry. Thirteen months. That's not so long. Besides, with the money I'll be able to send home, you and Tommy won't have to struggle so hard anymore."

"Noah, please. We don't want the money. We want you here with us. We'll find a way to make ends meet, just like we always have."

"I have to go Momma."

"But what if ..." Sarah began, but couldn't bear to complete the sentence.

"Somethin' happens to me?" Noah finished for her.

Sarah nodded, as tears began to pour down her face.

"Momma, nothin's gonna happen to me. Just keep me in your prayers and I'll be home before you know it."

Wiping her eyes, Sarah said, "Well, I wish you'd at least let us take you to the bus station in the morning."

"We've already been over this. Curtis is gonna do it, he'll be here at five a.m. sharp."

The next morning Noah was ready to leave an hour before his long-time friend was scheduled to arrive. After setting his suitcase out on the front porch, he quietly crept into his mother's room and kissed her softly on the cheek before whispering, "I love you Momma."

Then he walked over to the dresser and retrieved his father's ring from the box in the bottom drawer. Afterward, he went into the kitchen, poured himself a cup of coffee, sat down at the table and stared at the silver band.

He had taken it out of the box on a number of occasions since Noble's death, and had even memorized the Irish blessing. But he could never bring himself to put the ring on his finger. In fact, just holding it in his hand had the power to bring back the memory of Noble's face just before he hanged himself. That's what had happened the day his mother had given it to him, and that's why he didn't take it from her.

Now he planned to give it to Tommy for safe keeping. Hoping it would help him cope with his absence.

For several moments Noah stood over Tommy just watching him sleep. Then he nudged him and said, "L'il Bit, wake up. I want to talk to you."

Not long after, as the two of them sat out on the front porch waiting for Curtis. Noah held the ring out to Tommy and said, "L'il Bit, this ring belonged to Pap, and his pap before him. I want you to hang on to it until I get back. I want you to keep it safe for me. Can I count on you to do that?"

By the expression on Tommy's face, one would have thought Noah had just asked him to guard the most priceless treasure in the world. He looked at Noah seriously and replied, "I won't let anything happen to it Noah. I promise."

Just then Curtis arrived, and Noah and Tommy said their goodbyes. As the truck pulled away, Tommy slipped the ring onto his finger and whispered, "I won't let you down Noah. I promise."

In the province of the mind, what one believes to be true either is true or becomes true.

— John Lilly

Chapter Seventeen

August 31, 1968

For Tommy, life without Noah was nothing short of miserable. And now that Hannah had gone off to college, he felt completely lost and alone. To make matters worse, they had recently received a letter from Noah informing them that he had actually volunteered for another tour of duty in Vietnam. Tommy was beside himself at the news, and fell into a deep depression that Sarah could not seem to bring him out of. It was so severe, she was afraid he might even become ill.

For several weeks she agonized over rather or not she should write Noah of Tommy's progressively declining condition. In the end, she decided against it, because she knew he would become distracted with worry, and under his present circumstances, that distraction could cost him his life.

Not long after that, Sarah awoke one morning with a suffocating sense of dread. It was so encompassing, she found it difficult to get out of bed. Her first thought was that her worst fear had been realized, and her mother's intuition was telling her something awful had happened to Noah.

After dragging herself out of bed, she went to wake Tommy for school, only to find the cause of her dread right there in the house — Tommy had run away.

Lying on top of his neatly made bed was a note. It was short and to the point and simply said that he loved her very much and did not mean to hurt her, but he could not stay in Dawson any longer. The note also said he would write as soon as he got to wherever it was he finally planned to stay.

What sixteen-year-old Tommy chose not to include in the letter, was that if, by his estimation, he was lucky, his final destination would be South Vietnam.

As it turned out, obtaining false documents with a fictitious name that proclaimed him to be eighteen, proved easier than he had expected, and it wasn't long before he found himself freshly out of Marine bootcamp and on his way to Southeast Asia.

It broke Sarah's heart to think that Tommy had felt such desperation he had to run away. Once again, she turned to her old friend Ida Anderson for help, but even between the two of them, they could find no trace of Tommy.

Sarah prayed constantly that she would hear from him soon and that he was somewhere safe and sound. Again, she chose not to share this bad news with Noah. Although as week after week went by with still no word, Sarah realized she couldn't keep the terrible news from him forever. Finally, she was forced to write him about Tommy.

Noah did not receive the letter from Sarah until late November. As soon as he read the horrible news, he went straight to his commanding officer to request leave. It was granted immediately although it would be a week before he would be able to leave his post.

Two days after receiving the letter about Tommy's disappearance, Noah and his unit where out on patrol when they came across an overturned and burned out Deuce and Half. That was the name the military used to describe the two and a half ton, ten wheel truck used mainly for hauling troops. The truck appeared to have been blown off the road by some type of explosive.

As Noah and the other soldiers cautiously approached the vehicle with their weapons drawn, they communicated with one another with a series of hand signals and short, sharp whistles.

When they could find no sign of any soldiers in either the back of the truck or the cab, they silently spread out in pairs and began scouring the surrounding area. It didn't take long for one group of men to sound off with several high pitched whistles, signaling they had found something.

While several of the soldiers stood sentinel, in case the enemy was still in the vicinity, the others, including Noah, converged on the whistle blowers.

They had found the missing occupants of the Deuce and a Half. Judging by what was left of their uniforms, the men were American Marines. There appeared to be six in all, though it was hard to tell because their remains had been piled one on top of the other. All of the bodies were badly mangled, and all were missing their boots.

"McAllister, Fenton, and Lopez, you guys get a couple of tarps, lay these soldiers out in a row and cover them. Martin, you radio back to the base and have someone come out and pick these gentlemen up," Corporal Battery said, just above a whisper. Then he continued on with several other men who were scouting the area.

Jim Fenton headed back to the jeep for the tarps while Noah and Israel Lopez began laying out the bodies. After they had laid out the third one and were turning back to pick up the fourth, something caught Noah's eye. Bending down next to the unlucky Marine, he lifted up his right hand and looked at the ring on his third finger for several seconds.

Furrowing his brow, he took his finger and tried to wipe some of the blood off of it. Still not sure what he had or why it was so important, Noah removed the piece of jewelry from the soldier's hand, pulled out his shirt tail and began cleaning it off.

Israel turned around halfway between Noah and the remaining stack of bodies, "Noah, man, what're you doin'?" he asked in agitation.

All of a sudden, as Noah stared at the roughly carved silver band, with the etching of an "M" that only a McAllister would recognize as such, a gut-wrenching scream issued from the pit of his stomach. Then with his father's ring tightly clutched in his fist, Noah lost consciousness.

It took nearly five weeks for the Army to get the nearly comatose Noah transferred to a hospital closer to home. It was still a mystery even to the doctors as to what exactly had occurred that day in the jungle that caused Noah's mind to go AWOL.

Due to the super efficiency of the first medical technician to attend him, no one would ever connect the ring with his current condition. Because the first thing the technician had done, was to remove all of Noah's personal belongings including the ring, which he had had to pry from his clenched fist, and place them in a bag for safe keeping.

After a thorough investigation they could find no connection between Noah and any of the Marines killed that day who where just beginning their tour of duty.

The military doctors were extremely puzzled by Noah's condition. Physically, he was as healthy as a man could be. He could sit, he could stand, he could even walk. But he wouldn't speak, or acknowledge anyone's presence. And mentally, it was literally like the lights were on but no one was home.

The doctors kept him in the hospital for three months after his return stateside, hoping to find a solution that would cure him. They were unsuccessful. Finally, Sarah insisted on bringing him home.

As soon as Hannah found out that Noah was back in Dawson, she left school and immediately returned home to help Sarah care for him.

It warmed Sarah's heart to see young Hannah's unshakable dedication to her son. Ida and Ben were also regular visitors. Even as the days turned into weeks, and the weeks turned into months without any visible signs of improvement, they're support never faltered. And Sarah was grateful for that.

In all that time there was still no word from Tommy. So it was decided among Sarah, Hannah, Ida, and Ben, that when they were in Noah's presence, they would talk of Tommy as though he were simply away at school.

Nearly a year after Sarah had brought Noah home, they were sitting on the porch one day when a package arrived.

After signing for it, Sarah knelt in front of Noah and, as she began to open it, said excitedly, "Look Noah, you got somethin' in the mail." Then she turned the manila envelope upside down and dumped the contents into her hand — a Zippo lighter, one quarter, two dimes, and one roughly carved silver band, with an "M" etched into it, that only a McAllister would recognize as such.

Instantly realizing what the ring signified, Sarah closed her eyes in horror. Then she burst into tears and threw her arms around Noah. After several moments, Noah's shoulders began to shake as heartbroken tears flowed down his cheeks. Ever so slowly he reached out his arms and wrapped them around his mother.

Neither was sure how long they sat on the porch like that, pouring out their sorrow.

After that, Noah began improving little by little, day by day.

Shortly after the ring was returned to them, Sarah began making inquires regarding the recovery of Tommy's remains.

Nearly a month later, Sarah had just walked out onto the porch, when an official military vehicle pulled into the driveway.

Though she had been expecting this day, her heart twisted painfully in her chest.

The two men got out of car and started to walk toward her, one, she assumed was the Marine Chaplain, the other ... the other, Sarah couldn't put her finger on it but there was something hauntingly familiar about him.

The closer they got, the faster Sarah's heart began to pound. It wasn't until they were standing at the bottom of the steps that Sarah allowed herself to believe what she was seeing — Tommy! Her Tommy! Alive and well and standing right there in front of her.

"Noah! Noah come quick!" Sarah shouted.

A few seconds later, Noah threw open the screen door. His face turned as white as a sheet as he stood in the doorway, staring back at Tommy.

Tommy bounded up the few short steps and threw his scrawny arms around Noah. As the two hugged each other tightly, Sarah ran over and threw her arms around both of them.

"How is this possible?" She whispered, as the three of them continued to hang on tightly to one another.

"You didn't write. You didn't call. Where have you been?"

"Well, its a long story Momma, but we have all the time in the world for the telling ..."

EPILOGUE

As Sarah sat on the porch of her yellow house, while black velvet smoke from the red brick chimney curled up into the sky, a whisper of a smile lit up her face. She laid the book she was reading face down in her lap and closed her eyes.

A few moments later, when she heard a car pull into the driveway, she opened her eyes just in time to see a towheaded little ball of energy bounce out of the back seat and begin running full-tilt toward her.

As Noah got out and began helping Ida Anderson out of the car, the little boy shouted, "Grammy! Grammy! Look what I made ya!"

"Noble McAllister, slow down before you fall!" Hannah McAllister called after her rambunctious six-year-old.

Enveloping her grandson lovingly in her arms, Sarah said, "What is it?"

Noble held out a now crumpled, purple paper airplane.

Sarah took it from him and smiled broadly, "That's the prettiest thing I've ever seen. I'll treasure it forever."

Beaming with pride, Noble took off into the newly built house.

As Noah, Ida, and Hannah approached, Sarah said, "Is Tommy comin'?"

"Oh, he'll be here. I think Ben and he are coming together, maybe Curtis too," Noah replied, as his mother began to hug them one by one.

Before they had a chance to sit down, a police car pulled up behind Noah and Hannah's Buick. Two officers got out of the front, and Ben Hadley out of the back.

As Sheriff Curtis Hayfield, and Deputy Tommy McAllister began walking toward them, Noah laughed out loud and shook his head, "Whoever would've thought that?"

"What? That Curtis and Tommy would ever become part of Dawson's finest?" Hannah asked with laughter in her voice.

"Yeah."

"I would've," Ida said.

"Tommy, when are you gonna finally settle down and make a respectable woman out of that pretty Sandy?" she continued.

"Whenever she'll agree to marry me, Miz Ida," and then, "I sure hope Walt's bringing his famous chocolate cake."

"He wouldn't dream of showin' up here without it," Ida said, as Tommy hugged the adored elderly woman affectionately.

For a moment things turned serious as Tommy said, "Momma, they released the remains of Missy and Leonard to me yesterday for burial."

There was a long silence as those gathered recalled the recent trial of Ernest Tipton. The story in the paper read in part — due to an anonymous tip, Detective Mike Halverson, one of the original investigators in the nearly thirty-year-old murder case of Edna and Harvey Peterson, was able to recover the bodies of Melissa and Leonard Copeland. Two transients believed to be responsible for the brutal slayings of the elderly couple back in 1954.

In a surprise twist, the retired Sheriff of Dawson, Ernest Tipton, has been charged in the murders of Melissa and Leonard. After the bullet that killed Melissa was determined to have come from the gun that had been issued to the sheriff at that time ...

The article went on to say that Tipton's version of the events leading up to the crime could not be corroborated, and, despite his claims of widespread involvement by other Dawson residents, it was believed he acted alone. If convicted he would face life behind bars.

"I'm having them cremated tomorrow. No service. They didn't deserve it. Oh, by the way, it's official. My name is now legally

Thomas Sean McAllister. I got the documents in the mail today," Tommy finished on a happier note.

At the end of the day as the celebrations for the new house Noah had built for his mother came to a close, Tommy took Noah aside, handed him a book with the same title as the one Sarah had been reading earlier, and said, "Hey Mark Twain, can I get your autograph?"

Noah ruffled Tommy's hair and said, "Sure L'il Bit," then he opened the book, scrawled something in it, handed it back to Tommy and walked away.

Tommy flipped it opened to see what he had written.

It read simply, 'To the boy on the side of the road. Love, forever and ever and always, your brother, Noah.'